LIBERTY

V. J. Spencer

For my father-in-law.

The greatest man I never got to know.

CHAPTER 1

The body of Robert Brooker was discovered in the early hours of Wednesday morning on the 14th February 1976.

He was face-up on the grass in the back garden of his home, although what remained of his face was difficult to debate. Dressed entirely in motorcycle leathers, with a matching helmet still atop his head, it was probably deemed more respectful to leave him where he lay. His wife later found herself particularly thankful that the helmet was still in place. For when she reached down to check if her dear Robby was okay, she was shaken enough to find his hands stone cold, and the grass around him drenched red. She did not need to see the mess inside that helmet. The inspectors and police constables who attended the scene also agreed on this statement.

Mrs Brooker had been expecting her husband home the previous evening. He had rung ahead and told her he had to work late at the office – but that he would indeed be home by midnight. He had insisted over the phone that his wife put the children and herself to bed, as normal, and that he would join her later. First he had to finish up the paperwork that was insistent on being completed before the following morning. He had promised that the following day – being Valentine's Day – he would not be working late and wanted to ensure that he could give the entire evening to her. She was smitten, of course she was, and so had no issue with him being at the office a little while longer.

However, it was when she awoke at around 0400 hours that she was shocked to realise the time – and that the other side of their marital bed was as made-up as it had been when she fell asleep. Her hands searched in the darkness for him, and she found nothing and nobody except cold bedsheets. She had wandered the house, to check he had not simply fallen asleep elsewhere by accident – such as his armchair, or at the desk in his office – but unfortunately, he could not be found. It was only when, dressed in her robe and nightgown, she had entered the kitchen to make a phone call to his office, when she had looked out of the back garden, and seen the outline of a person laying on the grass. It was not Mrs Brooker that phoned the police, but instead the neighbours from number 39, the adjoining house, who had been awakened by the sound of her screaming.

Initially, the inspectors had assumed it was a form of suicide – it had been seen often enough. A stressed young man with a hard job and the pressures of family life, overcome with struggle to complete the façade, and so instead making a quick exit rather than battle on. But upon looking a moment more, the officers found no weapon in which they believed Mr Brooker could have successfully blown off his own face from underneath his motorcycle helmet.

"Foul play?" Elaine Brooker gasped between her sobs when the inspectors suggested it as a possibility. She was stood barefoot on the slabbed paving stones in the back garden, her face paler than an English rose. Her cheeks were flush and dampened from the tears. She was clutching her robe about her in the chill February morning air, whilst the three children sat on the back step to the house huddled under a blanket. Thankfully Mrs Guild from number 39 had joined her for emotional support. The elderly lady was rubbing Elaine's arm reassuringly, despite the action doing very little towards comfort, "But who could do such a thing? Who *would* do such a thing?"

"That, we do not know," The Inspector stated, coldly,

"And there is no way to know, just yet. Allow us time to gather some more evidence. Go inside and brew some tea. Change your clothes and tend to your children. We will be in shortly to question you further."

Mrs Brooker's bottom lip trembled so much that the inspector thought it might just fall off. She nodded solemnly, then turned to head back towards her home and her children, just as a huge sob erupted from her chest. She pressed the palm of her hand against her mouth to catch it, and it became a muffled whine. Mrs Guild from number 39 wrapped her arm around Mrs Brooker's shoulders and led her delicately back towards the house.

"Now, now, dearie," Mrs Guild said, as they stood in the kitchen, "You're frozen cold; I'll sort us a nice cup of tea, hey?"

Mrs Brooker took an incredibly shaky breath, seeming to be calming down, and nodded her dainty little head in agreement. Her blonde curls bobbed around her face. It appeared for a moment that she was going to do just fine. It seemed that the reassuring hands of Mrs Guild, and her grey hair and her gentle liver-spotted hands, had managed to make the situation almost as good as new. But just as Mrs Guild turned to find the tea leaves in the cupboard, Mrs Brooker's voice broke free once more, and she wailed a horrific wail that appeared to come from her very core. She sobbed and sobbed until her stance gave way beneath her. She found herself crumbled in a floral-clad heap on her black-and-white kitchen tiles. Mrs Guild was beside her, muttering words of reassurance and love, but Mrs Brooker could not hear her over the sound of her own cries. She was only a young thing, really, in the grand scheme of things. None of her children were above the age of eight years, and they would all now live their lives forever without a father. Little Lucy was only just two – it was doubtful she would even remember who he was.

"Oh dearie," Mrs Guild said, stroking her hair in a motherly fashion, "I am so sorry darling, I am ever so sorry, Elaine."

Apologies would do no good. Elaine Brooker felt the cold

black clutches of grief slink about her shoulders and encase her, and she lay back into them, trustingly. Her hair stuck to her neck where the tears had fallen, and for once she was not worried about where the curls fell, or that they were out of place, or that her neighbour had seen her in such an unsightly and disgraceful state.

Her husband was lying dead not twenty feet away in the back garden, his brains blown out inside his own motorcycle helmet. Nothing could stop her cries of despair, her shakes of fear, her gut-wrenching sobs that would surely have brought up her breakfast, had she eaten any.

Robert Brooker was murdered – no doubt about it.

CHAPTER 2

Mickey stood in front of the mirror in the gent's bathroom. With the comb his mother had bought him for his birthday some several years before, he combed back his silver hair, ensuring every strand was in the perfect place. The building was presently deathly still. He had arrived early for his shift, like usual. Mickey was many things – but he was never, ever late.

Many of his colleagues held a very relaxed approach to their working weeks. Arriving only a minute before they needed to – if that – with a uniform that was less than excellent. They often still displayed the crumples in it from where it had been haphazardly dropped on the bedroom floor the previous night, as opposed to being neatly folded, or hung up in the wardrobe with pride.

Mickey brushed down his bright red tunic and straightened one of the golden buttons as they gleamed at him in the mirror. It reminded him somewhat of the uniform he had worn when in the army – as brief a time as that had been. But rather than being a deep and muted green, the fabric was a perfectly pressed, gleaming, royal red. The gold embellishments really complimented it. He knew it was nothing compared to the honour that was looked upon those who served their country – but nonetheless, he was determined to wear it with pride. His work ethic was strong. No matter what his job, Mickey knew he would always do it to the best of his ability.

Of the people who worked within the building, Mickey guessed that he himself was the eldest – other than, of course, Olwyn, the lady who ran the concessions stand. Olwyn was also a character who arrived early for her work, to ensure that everything was in order in her little tuck shop before the customers began to arrive. It was a tiny little place really – nothing more than a glamorised cupboard with a hole in the wall – but she appeared to be quite happy in there on her own. Sometimes they would send in a younger person to assist her, if it was a particularly busy night. Olwyn never did really appreciate this. Those that were sent to help her had worked nowhere near her fifty-odd years of loyalty to the building.

Mickey exited the bathroom and waved to her across the lobby. At first, he didn't manage to catch her eye, as she was busying herself ensuring there were enough paper bags and bottles of fizzy pop, and that the popcorn machine was whirring itself to life in good speed. She polished the golden rim that lined the little serving hatch; and did so with such gusto and determination that Mickey, for a second, thought that she might wear a hole in the metal.

He called to her in his thick South-London accent: "Has it done sammin' wrong?"

She looked up from her work and laughed at him, displaying a warm smile filled with gapped teeth.

"You're certainly teachin' it a lesson!" He nodded, as he walked past.

"How're you today, Mouse?" She said to him, "The day treating you well?"

"Same as it ev'r does," He grinned at her, and headed through the heavy sound-proofed doors into the atrium, to complete his checks throughout.

Nothing can truly capture the feeling of standing, entirely alone, in an enormous theatre auditorium.

A room four stories tall. A room with rows upon rows

of seating. A room built to fit hundreds, if not thousands, of finely dressed individuals. Built with purpose for evening after evening of entertainment. Built to be filled with raucous laughter, or the rebounding waves of a standing ovation – pairs of palms beating against one another in gratuitous applause. A room built to captivate, to confuse, to allure, to surprise, to draw emotion from even the stiffest of all upper lips. This was Mickey's favourite place in the entire world.

He climbed the steps at the back of the atrium. It was a rickety metal fire escape that was hidden by some beautiful doors. He climbed it right to the very top. There in the Gallery, he walked down past the rows and rows of matching red-velvet seats, to the very centre, the very middle, and took his usual place in 36A. The railings here, just like in the rest of the building, were also golden. They had been beautifully polished by himself just yesterday afternoon. He folded his arms and rested his elbows upon the metal, leaning down. He allowed his eyes to take in the fantastic view before him.

The air felt electric – alive, almost. There was a buzz just beneath the surface. It was the aura of a place that was always ready, always waiting to be filled with life and imagination and wonder. This building was *made* to create on-stage masterpieces. And when that stage lit up later that evening, and the rest of the room would plunge into the darkest abyss. Only then would the building feel at peace with itself. Until that moment, it would forever hum and buzz and whisper and wait, ready for the performers. The room *needed* to be alive. It needed to be filled with the sound of a thousand heartbeats, and the whispers of excited breath.

Mickey loved to sit and soak up this feeling before his shift began. He loved to see the contrast of before and after. To feel the difference in the air. He loved to bring his own ham and piccalilli sandwich to work with him, wrapped in brown paper. Before his shift, he would always have a moment to himself to eat in peace, as he took in what was before him.

It was quite a rewarding job, really, working within a theatre. Although a thankless job, and one which required only the highest abilities of stealth and facelessness, Mickey found some of the greatest times of his life had been spent in that theatre, alone. His job was to greet the guests and show them to their seats. He would often walk people by the light of a torch to the restrooms should they require it during the show. His job was to ensure nobody tripped up the stairs or wanted for anything. He sold ice-cream during the interval, and removed anyone who was disrupting the performance for anybody else – be that through talking loudly or through drunken misbehaviour. Other than that, he and the other ushers were free to sit at the back of the auditorium, shrouded in darkness, and watch the show unfold, much like those who sat in the audience. However, unlike those that had dressed in their finest attire, and had paid for tickets weeks in advance, Mickey got to watch these first-class performances free of charge. In fact, he was *paid* to watch them. Sure, his seat was far less comfortable, and he may miss certain scenes of a play, or watch the same performance over and over for weeks on end. Repetitive and uncomfortable aspects aside, however, it was a fantastic perk.

After his sandwich was finished, Mickey proceeded to ensure all the fire exits were unlocked, and that each seat and its footwell were clean, spotless, and comfortable. He collected any lost belongings or bits of rubbish that had carelessly been neglected by the cleaning attendants after the previous performance. He worked his way down through all four tiers of the auditorium until he was right at the front, by the music pit.

All the house lights were on, and there was a magical, golden glow about the place. Mickey stood and stared upwards, up to seat 36A, where he had not long ago been sitting.

He brushed a crumb from his pristine uniform and stood up straight. What a fantastic evening, Mickey thought, and how lucky he was to be a part of it.

CHAPTER 3

The guests were all in their seats, all bubbling with musical giggles and whispers of excitement. All the gentlemen were dressed impeccably in their suits and bowties with pocket squares to match. Some glanced briefly at their wristwatches, trying their hardest to retain their nonchalant outward demeanour. In reality, they were just as eager as their female counterparts for the show to begin.

Mickey stood in the shadows, near to the entrance of the auditorium, in the Stalls. He had shown impeccable standards at his work, and so his manager had granted him the privilege of tending to those in the Stalls – those who were closest to the stage on the ground floor, with the best seats, and the most money.

"Excuse me," A gentleman said, catching Mickey's eye, "How long until the show is to start?"

Mickey checked his watch; "Approximately three minutes, sir," he answered. The voice had such manners that Mickey hardly recognised it as his own. The London twang that he had been gifted from childhood was replaced with a posh boy's voice that not even his own mother would have recognised.

"Ah, very good, very good." Said the man, and he settled back into his seat.

Just as promised, three minutes past and then an announcement was made over the loudspeakers that were dotted throughout the building: *Ladies and gentlemen, if you would please take your seats, this evening's show is about to commence!*

Mickey had heard the words so many times that he found himself muttering along with them under his breath. The same accent, the same tone, the same affliction as Mr Owen, the Front of House manager.

The lights went down, and the red velvet curtain drew upwards, and a captivating hush drew through the entire crowd, like a flame being extinguished by a candle snuffer. Mickey loved moments like that – they were magic. It was these small elements which really made a trip to the theatre memorable and exciting.

With the show under way, and with two other ushers visible from where he stood, Mickey took it upon himself to check that the lobby was clear. On occasion he would find latecomers would awkwardly scramble in, mid-performance, and disrupt the soft quiet that blanketed the audience. It reminded Mickey of a calm sea at night, with a big panicky sailboat in the centre of it – a lost couple trying frantically to get to their seats, whilst uprooting everything and everyone in their path. Whispers of "sorry – oh, I do beg your pardon!" were not relaxing and did not add anything whatsoever to the theatre-goers experience. He liked to check the lobby for sweaty people running in, so he could calm and quell them adequately before they entered the auditorium. Just because two geezers can't catch a taxi on time and ending up rocking up late shouldn't mean that the rest of the people on their row should have the magic broken for them.

"Alrigh' Olwyn?" Mickey said as he gently pressed the auditorium door closed behind him. With guests nowhere to be seen, his natural, London-heavy accent was free to roam. He walked with a gentle, charming swagger. Relaxed confidence that didn't boast.

"Bit of a crazy one, that were," Olwyn answered, from her little tuck-shop window, "it amazes me how such elegant ladies, dressed in their finery, can get like little kiddies when it comes to sweets! I all but ran out of liquorice allsorts – you would have thought the world was ending with the way one woman reacted!"

She laughed. It was a dry, quiet cackle that could have easily been mistaken for a wheezing cough. Her gapped teeth stuck out, but the crinkles round her soft eyes didn't make her appear like an evil witch from a fairy tale. Mickey was sure that, once upon a time, she would have been pretty. Age just hadn't treated her nicely.

Mickey however had been fortunate on that front. He was now nearing his mid-fifties and, despite not being over the moon about that fact, he looked rather dapper considering he had lived the years he had. His skin was not heavily-lined with wrinkles where gravity had dragged it down. His hair, although silver, was still thick and held firmly in place along his scalp. This was something he was incredibly proud of considering his own father had been balder than a cooked chicken. His top lip, too, was home to a neatly combed moustache that smiled or frowned whenever he did. He often found himself running his thumb and index finger along it when he was thinking, following the shape all the way down to his chin.

"They go barmey over a bleedin' bit ah sugar, din they?" He chucked back at her, "Any pear drops left, lav? I won't bite yer 'and off for em, don't you worry."

Olwyn did a little giggle, like she was a girl in a school yard, "I've always got some sugary treats spare for you, Mouse."

She was often flirtatious with him. Several of their colleagues had jested that the two should shack up together and live their very last days together within the theatre's walls. The thought of returning as a ghost did have an appeal. Mickey had been told several ghost stories of various beings that are believed to haunt the many secret rooms of the building. But the thought of waking each morning to Olwyn's smiley face – as lovely and friendly as she was – didn't excite him. At least, not in the way he knew it should, if marriage and commitment was on the cards.

Olwyn handed him a little paper bag, white with red stripes, filled with a small assortment of goodies that she promised "wouldn't be noticed" when it came to the next stock take. A few lemon sherbets, a couple of cola bottles, but several of his favourite – pear drops. He said how she was too good to him, far too good, and that he'd find a way to repay her. Then he gave her a cheeky smirk – one that pushed the left side of his face upwards, so he was winking at her as well.

"Oh, you are naughty," she'd laughed, and shoved him away.

It was amazing what a difference it made to an evening, having a pocket full of sweets. It didn't happen every shift, but Mickey found that the nights he had a pear drop tucked into his cheek were the ones that had an extra sizzle to them. He found they went a little bit more quickly, or that the actors said their lines with just that little bit more *umph* which made their performance top-notch. He sat at the back of the auditorium on his uncomfortable fold-down chair and sucked on the sweets one by one. He enjoyed being in the dark where nobody could see him. Mickey, although a confident chap, was not truly the type that wished to be the centre of attention. He was more the type that you could share a bottle of wine and a tasty conversation, rather than watch him stand before a crowd and command attention from others. His dreams had never stretched to being on stage. In fact, even standing on the stage to clean the sodding thing was enough to make him feel uncomfortable. At the back, in the dark, out of view, with a paper bag full of cola bottles. That was how it was, and that was how he liked it.

The most he could tolerate was at the interval. Ten minutes before the lights went up, Mickey and his fellow ushers would quietly disappear to the back-freezer-room and grab themselves a tray of ice cream. All were laid out ready for them by none other than Olwyn. The contraption was heavy, and most uncomfortable, but Mickey was used to the way it made his shoulders ache by this point. He would roll his eyes when the younger folk would complain about how heavy the trays were, and how the straps that wrapped over their shoulders would itch and stick into their necks. Mickey had done all that. His shoulders were strong enough. They had done it every night for several years.

"Quit yer moanin'," He'd say, "It'll all be over in ten minutes – not like yer the one buying the ice cream. Three pounds for a thimble of frozen milk? Robbin' bastards ain't they."

That would always make them laugh a little bit.

Then the house lights went up and the auditorium would quickly stir itself into a hubbub of life and laughter once more. Even more conversations and titillating banter echoed within the room than there had been before the show had begun. He took his tray and heaved it over his shoulders and proudly walked down to the front of the auditorium – where he'd see the gleaming brass and the rows of seats, all buzzing and moving like little bees in a hive. Not dissimilar to little children, they would each see him stood there with his ice cream tray and rummage in their pockets and wallets and purses to find some more pennies to dispose of that evening.

It did seem that the way these people had fun was by spending all the money they owned. They were always looking for the next thing to indulge in – be it an expensive pair of shoes, or a new tie, or a fabulous coat, or a ticket to the theatre, or a three-course meal before the show began, or a little bag of liquorice allsorts, or a tiny tub of ice cream. These people *loved* spending their money. Mickey was baffled that they had so much of it, and from where exactly they managed to find it all. Why did they wish to get rid of it so quickly? His paycheck was by no means meagre, but certainly would not allow him to frequent such places so often and live with such frivolity as the crowd seemed to. Tub after tub he managed to sell, and soon Mickey had managed to collect a sizeable amount of cash. Strawberry ice cream was the popular choice this evening. It wasn't long before he only had chocolate and vanilla. Ghastly stuff though. His thin bones didn't enjoy something so cold – even in an auditorium filled with warm bodies and a lack of ventilation.

"One vanilla, one chocolate," a man said. He approached, already rummaging in his wallet. It was brown leather with golden embellishment and stocked with more paper notes than Mickey had ever seen in possession of a single man. Mickey noticed how the man, although rich in money, did not appear to be rich in manners.

"Certainly, sir," He answered, with a winning smile, "That will be six pounds, please."

"Six pounds?" The man laughed, but it did not appear to denote humour, "You're kidding."

"Afraid not, sir," Mickey stood straight, stretching his shoulder blades from his heavy load, "If I was, I would have chosen a higher number!"

The man shook his head and leafed through his many notes once more. He didn't find Mickey's attempt at humour very funny. *Miserable fucker.*

He thrust the money into Mickey's hand and waiting impatiently to be given his ice cream and change. Purposefully, Mickey decided that he wanted to double and triple check he was giving the man the correct coins in return. He took his sweet time about it.

"Listen, old man," The man muttered under his breath, getting uncomfortably close, "I'm on an evening out with my wife. We have three kids at home, and she wanted an evening just me and her. Don't keep me waiting. I don't advise it."

"I'm just ensuring that everything is present and correct, sir." He replied, "I would hate to give you the wrong change."

Mickey made a point to not break eye contact with the man, who was so set on not blinking through his steely stare. Mickey counted the change without looking at it, put it on top of the two stacked ice cream tubs, and held it outwards.

"I believe it's all there, sir," He smiled, "I do hope you enjoy the rest of the show."

The man twisted his lip into a snarl. He snatched the items and marched back to his seat. Mickey watched him go.

It amused him. The man was well-dressed. A smart suit, slicked-back dark hair, and not an old man, by any means. He probably was not even thirty just yet. He said he had three children, and the wife that he spoke off, Mickey guessed, was the gorgeous young blonde that sat next to him, with a pretty smile and pin-up-girl worthy features. What would cause such a man, with such apparent fortune, to be so bitter and impatient, and call a stranger by unpleasant names? It amused Mickey greatly. It just reaffirmed his belief that having all the money and riches in the world was not, it would seem, the magical answer to all of life's problems. You could have the house, the money, the wife, the kids, the job, the clothes and the devilish good looks – and where did it get you? Complaining about the cost of chocolate ice cream and snarling in the face of a stranger. How strange. How sad. Olwyn would never do something such as that. Mickey doubted that the man's wife would do something like that either.

Mickey followed the man with his eyes as he stomped back to his seat and awkwardly rummage his way past the other guests. He handed the ice cream to his wife and then shoved his change into his trouser pocket. She looked ever so delighted and chatted to him as she patiently waited for him to sit beside her. She then handed him his ice cream and tucked into her own. He took it from her in a way that, to Mickey, echoed exhausted politeness. How unfortunate, he thought, that such a wonderful, patient, beautiful young lady, should end up with such an ungrateful man on her arm. Leading her in every dance, seeing it as a pain to bring her out of the house for the evening. Such a shame.

Mickey had never had such a lady, really. There was a girl, once, but that was a long time ago now, and it was not something that he wished to pursue again. Despite the attention he had received, and despite how Mickey *loved* women (very, very much indeed. There were few things he appreciated more in life than the silhouette of the female), he recognised that he did not have a mindset at present that a good lady would be looking for. He had little to offer, in the form of finances and support, and so knew that few fathers would see him as adequate marital material for their daughters. He was also no longer in the prime of his life and had spent those years doing many a thing that meant being a family man was not the easiest of promises to make. Sure, if the right girl came along, he wouldn't say no. And sure, if the right girl appeared to only exist for one night, he would never turn down a lady in need. But he would never go searching. They always seemed to find him. And, so far, it always seemed to be that they did not wish to request his company for more than a few nights at a time, before disappearing into the light of the rising sun the following morning. A shame, such shame. But life, for Mickey at least, was not intended to play out as it did do for most others. And he was fine with that. Everyone else seemed to always be wanting more. Mickey allowed things to find him, allowed opportunities to arise and then grasp hold of them when they did. He didn't struggle, he didn't fight. He just observed. And it had worked out pretty well for him for the past fifty or so years just allowing life to happen around him. It had not been easy, but he had found a peace, and he was quite comfortable to bathe in it a little while longer.

Little did he know, but his peace had other ideas…

CHAPTER 4

It was after the show. When everyone had left their seats and their rubbish behind, Mickey was cleaning the auditorium. He found it.

He had started at the top of the auditorium, right up in the gallery, and gone down each row, each seat, on his own. He collected the sweet wrappers and drink's cups and bottles as he went. Discarded, so thoughtlessly, by their posh guests. Mickey wondered if they did a similar thing in their homes before they had left for the theatre earlier that evening. He doubted it. As he also doubted there were individuals on a lower salary than they, dressed in red uniforms, following them around their own homes picking up after them.

He had worked his way down through the gallery, through the upper circle, and the lower circle, all the way down to the stalls. At about halfway, just off-centre from the middle, he bent down to pick up two empty ice cream pots. One vanilla, one chocolate. He popped them into the black bin liner he carried. Then, something gleamed from behind the seat, and caught his eye.

It was well-hidden. Clearly dropped, unnoticed by its owner. It was tucked right in the corner underneath the folding red seat. Mickey got down onto his knees and reached – sure enough, it was as he thought.

A brown leather wallet, with golden embellishments

around the edge.

He stood for a moment, just looking at it. It amused him.

Fackin geezer dropped his pennies, ey?

He opened it up, and looked inside; a few loyalty cards, a little pocket with some coins in it. A driver's licence for a Robert Brooker. Oh yes, the photo was certainly of him. Mickey recognised his face. He couldn't forget it, considering he'd stared at it without blinking for a good solid minute or two, only inches away from his own.

Out of nothing but curiosity, Mickey counted the bank notes that had been fanned under his nose earlier that night. His thumbs leafed through them, one at a time. It totalled to several hundred pounds.

The thought of anybody carrying such an amount on them in cash, at any given moment, appeared somewhat foolish to Mickey. Surely, in an event such as this, when the man had left his wallet behind, he was now not only missing a beautiful wallet, but also enough money to feed his family of five for a good few weeks!

Good at heart, Mickey knew the right thing to do. He motioned to his colleagues that he would be back shortly and left his bin bag where it was. He found Mr Owen and showed him the wallet.

"Ah, Mouse, this is wonderful news!" He said, "A gentleman was here not long ago asking about a wallet. If you run, you should be able to catch him!"

Mickey couldn't believe what he was doing as he was doing it. He steadily jogged down the cobble stone street alongside the theatre, chasing after a motorcar. His uniform would certainly be in need of a wash after this. His old knees protested at the solid, uneven surface he was running on – and at the fact he was running at all.

The motor he was following, luckily, slowed to a stop. As it did, Mickey did also, and doubled over to catch his breath.

The man got out of the red Beamer, the driver's side door. He stood and straightened his cuff links and slicked back his hair before closing the door and approaching Mickey. It was an unnecessary adjustment to his attire. Aside from the car's headlamps, the road was pretty much pitch black.

"Mr Brooker?" Mickey said, politely, "I believe I have found your missing wallet?"

The man didn't say anything, but snatched the wallet from Mickey's outstretched hand. He took out all of the bank notes and counted them, one by one, very steadily, very slowly.

"Good," He smiled, "It all appears to be present and correct..."

He then opened the coin pocket within the wallet and tipped the contents into his opposite hand. Again, he counted. Mickey stood before him, in disbelief.

"Not a penny missing. Now that *is* a surprise," Mr Brooker smirked, "Here; take this for your trouble and good heart."

Robert Brooker held out a fifty-pence-piece.

"Keep yer fackin' pennies ya ungrateful cant," Mickey said. It was a harsh sentence, but it was not spoken loudly, "Yer better watch yerself, you 'ad."

"Suit yourself," Mr Brooker replied, and he held out the coin over an open gutter in the road and dropped it. It clattered over the metal railings before falling through them, into the water below, with a quiet *plop*. Gone forever.

Mickey stood and watched as Mr Brooker returned to his lovely red BMW. He shushed his lovely blonde wife who was in the passenger seat, who was no doubt asking questions about their exchange of words. He revved the engine, a sound that was far louder in the dead of night than it would have been amidst the busyness of the daytime. The deep roar echoed off the sides of the buildings and the cobbled street, and the pair disappeared down the road, into the night.

Mickey stood alone, his knees aching and his previously-neat hair flopping to one side. He was speechless, and breathless, and couldn't believe what had happened. He kicked himself for not keeping the blasted wallet all to himself. It was the carelessness of its owner which had led to it being lost in the first place, after all.

Looking up at the deep blue-black of the sky above him, and the twinkly stars, and the beauty of the world and how quiet it was, Mickey made a silent prayer. He was not often a religious man, did not go to church on Sundays, did not keep a Bible by the side of his bed – couldn't even remember how many disciples that Jesus bloke had. But on this night, he made a prayer to whomever was listening up above. He prayed that Robert Brooker would get what was coming to him. He prayed that Robert Brooker would see his comeuppance. He prayed that Robert Brooker would see the dark and grizzly end that he deserved.

Mickey nodded to the sky, as if the deed was already done. He then lit a cigarette, and breathed in deeply, before walking a steady and thoughtful walk back the way he had come.

CHAPTER 5

The thuds on the front door were certainly going to take it off its hinges if Mickey didn't get out of bed and answer it soon – he was sure of it.

"What's wi' that fackin' racket?! Quiet, will ya?!"

He staggered out of bed, delirious. What was the time? He checked the alarm clock by the side of his bed and noticed that the little hand was pointed toward the six. Whatever was going on, it was far too early to be waking him up.

He thanked himself for putting on his navy-blue pyjamas, and for not sleeping in a vest and boxers, as he so often did. It had been cold the night before – February could still throw some chilly weather around, despite Spring being just around the corner.

Thud-thud-thud!

"ALRIGH' I'M CAMIN'!" Mickey bellowed at the door, as he tried to dig his arm into his dressing gown, and shuffle into his slippers. His keys fumbled in his slender fingertips, "This better be fackin' important…" He muttered.

He said a few more curse words under his breath as he undid the locks and the bolts and the chains on the door. The early-riser that stood waiting on the other side gave another sharp *rat-tat-tat*. Mickey felt about ready to hurl them straight down the hallway.

He undid the last latch. He swung the door open. Before

him stood a young man, in very smart clothes, with a scraggly beard on his chin and moustache to match around his mouth. The dark hair on his head was swept back, very smartly, and on his face, he had a great big grin.

"Mouse, guess where I've just come from."

"You fackin' bastard. You woke me up for a game of *Twenty*-fackin'-*Questions*?"

"I'll give you a hint," The lad said, unphased by the profanity, "It wasn't my house."

"I bloody guessed that, di'n I?" Mickey said, "You got the same clothes on you did yesterday." His tone softened, and he gave a proud smirk, "You better come in, I s'pose."

The lad beamed and practically skipped into the flat. He pushed past Mickey, as he re-bolted the door, and waltzed into the living room where he placed himself down on the sofa as if it were his own. Up went his feet onto the coffee table, and out of his pocket popped a cigarette. He had lit it and was taking a long exhale before Mickey was sat down opposite him.

"Getcha feet dahn," Mickey said, as he took a cigarette from his companion's outstretched hand, "I've told you before; I put my biscuits on there. Treat my 'ouse with a bit of respect, will ya?"

"Sorry, Mouse," The lad answered, and promptly swept his feet down, crossing one ankle over the opposite knee, "I'm just giddy. Giddy as a schoolboy!"

"Come on then, Marcus, out with it," He jested, "Tell me about her."

He took a deep drag from his cigarette, "She's perfect."

"Bollocks. No such thing."

"It's true!" He leant forward, and Mickey could see his eyes were filled with a wonder that they had certainly never been filled with before. True to his word, he certainly did look like a schoolboy. It was as if he'd just seen a magic trick for the first time and couldn't understand what he was seeing, but certainly believed it, "She's beautiful and she's funny and she's smart – she's been to university!"

Mickey nodded with an impressed frown, "She does sound like something special," he acknowledged, "What's she doin' hangin' out wi' a munter like you then?"

The two shared a smirk.

"*Well*," he said cockily, "I think you'll find she described me as *charming* and *witty* and said that she had a wonderful evening *and* would like to see me again."

"Right, I hear you there, loud an' clear," Mouse said holding his hands out in surrender. He took another drag from his cigarette, "But here's my question: if you had such a great night together – and I presume you stayed over?" – the lad nodded with a grin filled with pride – "why the fack are you bangin' on my front door at 'alf past six in the fackin' mornin'?"

Marcus laughed, "You crack me up you do," He said, "She kicked me out! I wish I could say I sneaked out without her noticing and that I didn't wanna see her again – get in, get off, get out kinda deal – but it's not like that with her! She woke me up at like five or something and said she had some fitness class to go to before her lecture at nine. Told me to get up and get out! And that she'd call me."

"Ha!" Mouse got up from his sofa and chuckled to himself as he walked over to the kitchenette to fill up the kettle, "If you were a lass tellin' me this tale, I'd tell you to keep your expectations low. Never heard of a girl kicking a guy out of her bed!"

"It's unheard of, right?" Marcus sounded incredibly delighted by the thought, "She's just so surprising and-and...*different*! I love it! So many girls are just clingy and whiney and just want-want-want and nothing's good enough. Remember that girl I went out with a couple months back? What was her name?" he clicked his fingers in the air, as if trying to will the name into existence.

"Katlyn?"

"Nah, the other one."

"Joanne?"

"No, no...it was..."

"Elizabeth?"

"Elizabeth! Yeah, her. She was a right piece of work! I swear the only two things we did when we were together were fuck and argue. It was insane! One minute she'd be all over me, the next she'd be shoving me about and screaming in my face. It was insanity!"

"Girls *are* insanity though, Marc," Mickey grinned, fondly, as he got out two mugs and popped a tea bag in each of them, "Can't live with 'um, can't live without 'um. That's the beautiful thing about them – hypnotic and abusive, all in one." He spooned in the sugar, waiting for the kettle to tell him when the water was done. "This girl you saw last night – you sure she's not a psycho as well?"

"I'm certain."

"Then I know one thing for sure."

"Yeah?"

"She's gonna drive you fackin' nuts."

Mickey perked up after he'd had his first brew of the day – even if it was much, *much* earlier in the day than he would have liked. He didn't remember what time he'd gotten home the night before. After finishing work, it felt like the trip home had passed without his noticing, because before he knew it, he was wrapped up under the blankets, his uniform neatly folded ready for the next day, and his jaw gently resting open as he snored away his fatigue. If it weren't for his late nights, Mickey would probably class himself as a morning person.

Mickey's bleary eyes looked over the rim of his mug. No matter what the time, Marcus was always happy company. The two had known each other for years. The kid had started out as the local paper boy and they'd exchanged chit-chat every now and again. Then as the years passed and the boy got older, Mickey had managed to get him a job at the theatre alongside him. Now, Marcus was doing something to do with motors; selling them or renting them out or fixing them or something; they rarely discussed the nature of the work he did. They mostly just talked about the motors themselves and the makes and the models and the sound of the engines, and the issues that they had.

Mickey loved motorcars. Always had done, always would do. His blood was made of petrol, and his stomach-acid diesel, he would joke. He remembered when he was a youngster, he'd entered the football pools on a one-off and, against all odds, had actually gone and won. Aged nineteen it was more money than he'd ever heard of in his life and so he did the only thing that a nineteen-year-old could think of – bought seven brand-new sports cars. His mother had come home that afternoon, gotten off the bus and commented: "Oh, it would appear someone in the neighbourhood is 'avin' some sort of party."

"Nah mum, they're mine."

Goodness knows how she didn't whack him round the earhole for pissing his money away like that.

Nowadays, Mickey was reminiscent of those cars. He now no longer owned a single one. Life had come and gone, and he'd sold them or had them stolen. That area of London in which they lived was not exactly the safest of places. Mickey moving away from the city wasn't really a choice of his own, but he certainly knew that where he was now was a safer neighbourhood.

Marcus and Mickey sat for a few hours. They sipped their tea and smoked their cigarettes, and after a while Marcus made the two of them bacon sandwiches with some Heinz ketchup, to set the two up for the rest of the day. Mickey told Marc about the arsehole customer he'd had to deal with at work. Marcus spoke more of the girl he was, oh-so-clearly in love with.

"I'm not in love," Marcus insisted, shaking his head.

"No?"

"No. I can't be in love. I'm too young. Plus, just cause she's great doesn't mean we're gonna get married and that. We've only been on, like, two dates."

"Two dates and she let you stay over? Sounds like love to me." He elbowed him, playfully.

The lad laughed, "Yeah, it was amazing. Dirtier than she comes across."

"When are you seeing her again, then?"

"I don't know, honestly," He frowned, "When she calls me, I guess?"

"You don't have her number?"

"No, she never gave it to me."

Mickey laughed again, "She really is mysterious, this one. You sure she wants to see you again?"

He ignored him, "I know what classes she's got today. I'll be able to see her if I wanted to. I just don't wanna, y'know, crowd her too much. I don't wanna scare her off."

"Because you *lav 'er,* ain't that right?"

Marc shook his head with a smirk as he stood up from the sofa, "Right – I'm off. We can debate this later on. I gotta get to work. What have you got planned for the rest of the day?"

"I don't really have any plans – apart from work tonight," Mouse shrugged, "Back again, same performance. Some play about an inspector and some geezers getting locked in a hotel during a snowstorm, or sammit. Guess we'll see what the day brings me."

They said their goodbyes and shared a handshake and pats on the back. Mickey showed him to the door. To both of their surprise, when they opened it, there was already somebody stood behind it. Two somebodies, in fact.

"Michael Donaldson?" The first one asked.

"Who's askin'?"

"My name is Police Constable Ben Warner, and this is my colleague, Police Constable James O'Reilly. We have some questions we'd like to ask you about the recent death of a Mr Robert Brooker."

CHAPTER 6

Marcus remembered the first time he had ever met Mouse.

He was twelve years old and it was raining that day. He'd been in his job as a paper boy for only a couple of weeks by that point. He was a driven young man and was determined to do the best for himself in life. He wanted to buy new Poké-mon cards, but his mum wouldn't get them for him. So, using strong initiative, he'd gotten himself a job.

He cycled down the street with his huge bag of news-papers strapped to his back. As he cycled, he threw the papers, one by one, onto the doorsteps of the houses. The entire street was dressed in a veil of grey from the clouds above. The rain was ceaseless. It was that rare sort of rain that refused to let up and pelted him on the back as he cycled. He was wearing a raincoat but might as well have not bothered. His dark hair was sod-den, like he'd just had a bath. His jeans stuck to his thighs and weighed heavily around his legs, making it difficult to cycle. The denim chaffed behind his knees. He could hardly see where he was going.

He went back to the newsagents after he'd done his deliv-eries, and parked his bike up outside, leaning it against the win-dow. He'd gone inside and collected his monies from the shop owner – a man who really didn't care about his existence what-soever. In later years, Marcus couldn't even remember the man's name.

The bell sounded as young Marcus exited the shop. He saw two teenagers surrounding his bike where it rested against the shop window. They had hoods up, so Marcus could not see their faces. They looked at the bike and tipped it up from its tilt from off the window, admiring it.

"Erm, hi?" Marcus was unsure what else to say.

"Shove off."

Marcus stood, confused. The teenagers wheeled the bike away from the window. One of them swung their leg over it.

He took a step towards the boys and placed a hand on their arm: "That's my bike."

"Not anymore."

"But –"

"I said, *shove off*."

The teenager on the bike pushed him and did so with enough force that Marcus slipped and ended up on the floor. The shop bell dinged again behind him. Marcus didn't notice. He was already soaked, so the fact he ended up in a puddle didn't faze him.

"Oi, dickhead," Marcus said, with more confidence, as he pulled himself to his feet, "I said *that's my bike*."

The boys laughed and began to walk away. Marcus went to follow them but was then surprised when a slender figure in a black fleece jacket walked past him. He had a trilby hat upon his head, also black. Although he wasn't tall or broad really, in any way, he walked with the confidence of a man who demanded respect. He held an umbrella in his hand, in a very tight grip, but did not have it up, protecting him from the rain.

The man walked behind the two boys and took hold of the back of the bicycle seat. They were forced to a halt.

Through the rain, Marcus watched the three figures. To begin with, the teenagers appeared aggressive. They spun around and both stretched their necks and twitched their shoulders as if they were making threats. But then the man pointed a finger at them and said something in a low voice that

Marcus couldn't hear. The raindrops pelted onto the pavement. Marcus stood clenching and unclenching his fists, not sure of what to do. The teenagers, in unison somehow appeared to lose height and stance with the more words the man said. They withdrew into themselves, like snails into their shells, and hung their heads. Then, one of the lads – the one with the bicycle – dismounted and walked it back to Marcus.

"Sorry," he mumbled, and handed it to him.

Marcus did not say thank you.

The boys then disappeared – and did so quickly.

"You alrigh', kid?" The man asked, as he approached.

"Yeah," He answered. Looking through the rain, Marcus couldn't see where the teenagers had gone. He couldn't remember ever seeing their faces. "Thank you, sir."

"What's yer name?"

"Marcus."

"Right Marcus, if those bastards give yer any trouble again, you tell 'um you know Mickey Donaldson. And if that don't bother 'um, tell 'um that if they don't leave yer the fack alone, you'll take their fackin' stupid baggy trousers and pull 'um up so far that it'll rip their arseholes in two."

Marcus smiled and nodded.

The man opened up his umbrella and placed it above the two of them for a bit of shelter; "Shit weather, ain't it?" He used his shoulder to rest the umbrella while he unwrapped a new packet of cigarettes, "You gon' be alrigh' gettin' home?"

"I should be sir, thank you."

"See you 'round, Marcus."

"You too. Thank you again, Mr Donaldson."

"It's Mickey. Mr Donaldson was my dad. And he was a fackin' cant if ever there was one."

Marcus had found that funny. He'd not known an adult to ever swear so freely. He got on his bike and rode away.

An unlikely friendship. But a good one.

As Marcus did not have the greatest relationship with his own father either, Mickey had become somewhat of a role model. There was little in it for either of them, but the two were without the company of others the majority of the time – and this was something that, surprisingly, meant they spent more time together.

Marc grew into quite an extraordinary man. He followed the examples he'd seen from Mickey where he could but struggled with the aggression that he was confronted with at home. His dad was someone he'd met, but only a handful of times. He'd show up at odd birthday parties and the occasional Boxing Day. It was never planned. Marc never was aware of it beforehand. He just showed up, unannounced, usually with a gift that really had very little thought put into it. He was estranged by his own choosing. He just liked to pop into Marcus's life to shake things up whenever they got too "samey".

Marc's mother on the other hand, was...a tricky one, too. She was loving and had always wanted children. But being a single mother, working incredibly hard, with a husband who was so rarely around that years could pass between meetings – it put a strain on her, and it made her lash out. More often than not, verbally. Sometimes, with her hands. She would lock Marcus in his room and starve him, if it was a really bad day for her. Marcus had hated her as a child and had ran to Mickey's house for shelter and for comfort. Mickey was fully aware of the situation. He allowed the boy to stay on the sofa, as Mickey did not possess a spare room. But he always checked his mother knew where he was. She always seemed very grateful for the break – but acted as if her son was nothing but trouble.

People do not seem to realise that children really do become the things they are repeatedly told they are. They are moulded from the grooves that their elders and siblings create for them. When Marcus hit his teenage years, he became aggressive and violent and anti-social. He never touched anyone who didn't ask for it. But he was often in a fight, and often knocked on Mickey's door with a bloodied nose or lip and bruised and scraped knuckles. He slept less and looked waxy white, with large dark circles beneath his pale eyes – from deprivation from his bed, or from his most recent scuff, it was hard to tell.

Mickey worried for him but kept his input minimal. Usually when he asked to hear the story behind Marc's latest scar, it was never him that started it. The kid was just unlucky when it came to school friends.

Luckily, after he left school, and after getting a job at the theatre, his visions of red seemed to cool. Mickey was sure to teach him lessons he had learned himself throughout life. Tidying up after himself, how to tie a tie, how to iron a shirt, or cook himself a meal that included vegetables. He taught him the *proper* way to hit someone – thumb on the *outside* of the fist, not the inside – but also, when to hit, and when to walk away.

Mickey was certainly on a pedestal in Marcus's mind, but it was a well-earned place. As much as it unsettled him to have someone look up to him so much, Mickey did not shake it. He recognised that the lad had nothing else to guide him. He was afraid of what might happen should Mickey wander too far off ahead, in his own life. He cared for the boy, and worried for him. He was proud to watch him grow into a man who could hold down a job, and who had repeatedly said "no" to drugs, despite being offered them by multiple groups.

Throughout all these years however, Marc had not once seen Mickey under any sort of real pressure. He'd never seen him lost for words, ashen in the face, or vulnerable. In his eyes, Mouse was invincible.

So, on this morning, stood beside him in the hallway of his little flat, as he answered the door, it was strange to watch Mickey's face fall. It was strange to see that inquisitive eyebrow and that charismatic smirk drop into a frown.

"May I come in?" The police officer asked again.

Mickey stood, motionless, blinking rapidly. He looked very confused.

Marc gave him a nudge, "Mouse?"

"Yes – sorry – yes, yes..." He moved to one side, and the two officers walked past, into the living room.

"I'll stay." Marc said, squaring his shoulders and eyeing up the two men that now stood in the living room.

"No, son," Mickey said, quietly, "I don't think you'll be allowed to listen in."

"But –"

Mickey opened the front door wider, "I'll catch up wi' you later."

Hesitant, Marcus stepped out into the hallway and glanced at the floor. The carpet was well-worn and beginning to fray – deep red colour, embellished with a hideous green pattern. By the time Marc looked back upwards again, the front door to Mouse's flat was closed shut.

CHAPTER 7

Four weeks earlier...

F elix wasn't his real name. But Felix was the name he went by.

His arms were tanned and decorated. When he rolled up his sleeves, he revealed forearms possessing artwork of a tiger with a bleeding heart in its mouth. A snake wrapped around a dagger. A wolf's eyes that mirrored the face of a screaming child.

Resting against his ribs, on both sides, were two hand pistols. Tucked into a leather carrier, hidden beneath his jacket. They weren't his weapon of choice but were certainly the most convenient of things to carry with him. Concealed, just in case. He wasn't looking for trouble tonight – but that didn't mean he wouldn't find it.

The street he walked down that night was not well-lit. It was lined with several small groups of people. The quiet and the dark that drew this type of crowd – dark corners allow for risky business to go unnoticed.

Men in expensive coats, and women dressed in what can only be described as modest lingerie. Belly buttons on show, and thigh-high boots that revealed just the top part of their thigh, nothing else of their leg. For some reason, that part of a woman's leg is the sexiest.

As Felix walked, a man caught his eye. A man who was broader than he was tall. He wore a deep blue suit and no tie, with his collar undone and unattractive chest hair rumbling out from beneath the cotton.

"Your usual, Felix?" He asked in a gruff and tar-lined voice. The redhead on his arm fluttered her long eyelashes at him as she looked him up and down, approvingly.

"Not tonight, Jerry. I'm here on business, not pleasure."

"Pity," The lady purred.

She reached out as Felix passed, and caressed her hands down the sleeves of his leather jacket. He smirked. She went by the name of Spark and she certainly did know how to ignite a flame. If the evening went well, he would return later and see if she was still available...

The street that he walked down was littered with tins and old newspapers and other bits of junk. Here and there, he could see oil drums erupting with flames. Their sole purpose was to keep the local drug addicts warm, so they didn't die of frost bite in between fixes. Looking after your clientele was just common sense. Felix looked at them with little sorrow in his heart. He played the game, but he didn't let it beat him – that was the trick. He always stayed in control. He had built a life where he had a roof over his head, food and warmth. Anything else was a luxury. He ruled the drugs. The drugs did not rule him.

As he walked, people stepped aside for him and nodded their heads as a form of recognition and respect. They knew who he was, even if they had never been formally introduced. This was Felix's land. He was not born there, but he had eagerly made it his home. King of the Outcasts, some had said. It was not a noble title. But it was the nicest of all the names that Felix had ever been called.

Felix took a left down an alley – one without any drug addicts. The brick walls that lined it had been attacked by the eager hands of street artists. He used the term "artist" very loosely here. Sure, there were some good pieces of reptiles or ladies' cleavages – even one very good portrait of a cartoon clown.

It had crazy swirly eyes and a tongue that was wrapped around several bottles of vodka. Very clever stuff. But the rest of it was just nobody's claiming they had been there or writing down their telephone numbers should a passer-by ever be in need of "a good time". Felix knew for certain that if ever he personally *did* want a good time, he would not be taking the number off a wall in the back alley of a gentleman's club. He would choose a companion whose face he had seen, before talking to them – or even skipping the hellos and getting straight to the fun part, as some instances had gone.

There was a single bouncer on the back entrance to the club. It was not an entrance that was often, if ever, used.

"Gary," Felix said, with a nod.

"Felix," the nod was returned. As if using the man's name was the password, the door was opened for him.

The club wasn't especially loud, but the bass beat could be heard from outside the building, just about. Felix emerged into the room from behind a velvet curtain made of deep purple material. It was used only to disguise the entrance and to make the interior of the club look more expensive.

The walls and furnishings carried this colour theme throughout – deep purples, lilacs, and pale blues. There were several platforms. Some stand-alone, and one larger one in the centre of the room, with metal poles that stretched all the way from floor to ceiling. Each had a young and attractive woman swinging off it, or seductively removing a piece of her clothing as she danced. Felix's eyes scanned the room. They saw each the ladies in turn but did not hold onto them.

There, sat in a quiet corner, being straddled, was the man he had come to see.

Felix walked with conviction but didn't rush. The other gentlemen in the club didn't even notice he was there. They were far too caught up in the entertainment and eagerly giving their money away. It was the sexiest form of charity that had ever existed. Or the cleverest form of robbery. Who could say?

"Here you are, love," Felix said, as he approached the lady

that was doing the straddling and shoved a large pound note into her hand, "now clear off."

The man stayed seated as the young lady jumped off him and scuttled away. He wore a pale grey suit – *with* tie. That's how you could tell the difference between people around here.

"You," Felix said to the man, "Come with me."

He didn't look back to check that the gent was following him. They always did.

The two men walked towards the furthest wall of the club, leaving the bass beat and the bouncing breasts behind them, and exited into a back room. It was dark and didn't have such lavish furnishings as the club itself did. The room had simply been painted the same shade of pale blue, on each wall. They must have just had leftover paint. There was a circular table and six chairs that resembled the uncomfortable brown plastic ones that schools always had too many of. There was one source of lighting – a bulb that hadn't been dressed with a lampshade. The light was bright and bounced off every wall.

Felix helped himself to a seat, then grabbed another to prop his feet up on. The two scraped on the floor with an unpleasantly loud screech. He gestured to his companion to join him, which he did so promptly.

"You have a bit of attitude, I see," the man said.

"If that surprises you, you clearly don't know enough about me," Felix was unimpressed, "I don't mess about. Let's get to it. Word is you wanna make a deal with me."

"What you've heard would be correct."

The man smiled. It was an unpleasant smile. In any other circumstance it might be misconstrued as charming, or even dashing. But in this lighting, in this room, in this circumstance – not so much. With the way that the light cast dark shadows under his eyes and cheekbones, it was a menacing smile. Dark, but without much volume.

Felix looked the man up and down. Rob was his name, apparently – or that's the name he went by. That's all Felix knew. He was very smartly dressed, his grey suit and dark blue tie impeccably ironed and all in place. His shirt was tucked in. He sat with a posture that was relaxed, yet still strong. His face was clean shaven, not a single razor-bump or nick in sight. His dark hair was slicked back and well combed.

Felix was unsure whether or not he could trust this man, just yet.

"What is it that you want from me then, exactly?"

"I heard you know everyone around here?" It was posed as a question. Fact-checking.

"There isn't anybody I can't get hold of." Felix said, re-phrasing to make the statement correct, "Who is it you need?"

"Well, that's the thing. There's someone I very much *don't* need. I need them getting rid of, if that's possible?"

Felix squinted as he listened. He made sure to never agree to anything, in any degree, before he was certain he wanted the job. Even on weeks when money was tight and jobs were desperately needed, Felix was always sure to display a demeanour that came across as aloof, uninterested, thoughtful. He never, ever, gave too much away.

"Continue." He said.

"I've got a bit of a business going, you see," He went on, "I've started dabbling in a few trades and found I'm quite good at it, despite only being a few years into it. The thing is, there's a person who keeps getting in the way, getting a little too close for comfort, who I think is a bit of a threat to my potential success. Do you see what I mean by that?"

"You've got someone who's not into all this dodgy shit who keeps shoving their nose in where it's not wanted. And you can't trust that, if they did find out, that you'd be able to get away with it, 'cause they'd rat you in."

"You got it."

"How much are they against illegal activities?"

"Very."

"Authoritative? Or Goody-two-shoes?"

"The latter."

"Hm..." Felix thought for a long moment. He rummaged

in his pocket and brought out a box of pre-rolled cigarettes. He offered one to his companion, but the offer was declined. Felix brought out his zippo lighter and looked at Rob through the flames.

"Alright," He said, "Tell me more about them. Who is he? Where's he live? What's his name?"

"Well this is the first thing I should tell you, Felix," Rob laughed with a polite smile. He briefly scratched the end of his nose, "It isn't a *'he'.*"

Felix sat back in his chair again, "No problem. Women can be ever so meddlesome without even trying. Who's the bird?"

"A Mrs Elaine Brooker." The man said, "She's my wife."

CHAPTER 8

Mickey sat alone in his living room. It was dark now. He'd forgotten to turn any of the lamps on as the day ended. He'd been sat there all afternoon. Due to it still being February, the nights hadn't lengthened, so it wasn't late. But still. He had spent all afternoon sat there, in his pyjamas and dressing gown and his little slippers, clutching a mug of tea that had now gone stone cold.

Murder?

The police had asked him many questions. They'd asked him to recount everything from his evening at work, everything that happened before he'd even gone to work, and everything after. Mickey told them, as best he could. He had done the same as he always did, as far as his head could recall for them.

He thought about the prayer he had made that evening, and how he had wished death upon a man that was now lying in a morgue somewhere, wrapped in the medical equivalent of a bin liner.

He debated whether or not he wanted to take back his prayer.

He debated for a very, very long time.

CHAPTER 9

Elaine Brooker had originally been Elaine Ascot.

She was a lady who had grown up in a well-to-do household. Her father was a banker. Her mother was a seamstress, but mostly just for fun. They had housekeepers that assisted with the chores and the keeping things clean. Being a lady of leisure, Mrs Ascot liked to keep herself busy. She would fix and create garments for her friends, extended family, and occasionally people from the local neighbourhood.

Elaine had done well in school. She was not the smartest, but she was intelligent. She'd always achieved Bs or above in all of her tests, and at parent-teacher evenings, her teachers had expressed their contentment with teaching such a well-mannered young girl. She would never have classed herself as popular, but at the same time there was not a single person in school who had an issue with her. When she walked through the corridors, people said hi to her. She was never purposefully tripped by a bully and was never picked last in netball when it came to picking teams.

Things even went well after she finished school. She got a job at first helping her mother with her seamstress business, but it was not quite Elaine's idea of fun. She enjoyed reading and learning and yearned for her schooldays even years after she had finished her final year. That was what had led her to taking up a job as a teaching assistant, and training to become a teacher for children in primary schools.

The act of gifting knowledge to younger generations and assisting children with learning how to spell and read and write and explore their own creative minds – it was very fulfilling work for her. She loved it. She worked every day up until the day she left for her maternity leave, when she was expecting her first child.

Elaine had always thought that she would make a good mother. She had never really had experience growing up with younger people. She had no younger siblings (or older siblings, for that matter), nor did she have any cousins. But the moment she held her son in her arms for the first time, she felt a pull inside of her that was stronger than she ever realised it could be.

She had shared a moment with her husband, and their little baby boy, in the stillness of the master bedroom in their home. He hadn't wanted to be in the room for the birth, but the midwife had gone to fetch him when she was certain everything was okay. Robert had emerged, curious, but calm, from behind the doorframe, and walked the short distance between there and the four-posted bed. Elaine was bundled modestly beneath the duvet and the blankets, and their son was bound in a protective bundle of soft white towels.

Robert had stood over the two of them and looked into the eyes of their son.

"I was thinking of calling him Christopher," she said, "after my father."

Robert's face was stern as he thought, "Hm. Possibly." He said.

"Would you like to hold him?"

"Not right now, darling. This is a very expensive suit and I still need to attend that meeting at work, later this afternoon. He's charming though, isn't he?"

"He's handsome, just like his father."

The two shared a lovely smile together and he bent down and gave her a kiss.

"Would you be able to make me a cup of tea please, darling?" she asked.

"I'll ask the midwife if she can do it. I need to go. Goodbye, honey."

And with that, her husband was gone, back to work, like he normally was. He spent an awful lot of time at work, especially lately. As soon as Elaine and he got married, it was as if a drive was ignited within him to fine resources for the two of them, and their growing family. He was always trying to find new ways to make money and always spending longer and longer hours at the office. Elaine didn't mind, of course, because she understood that he was only doing it for her, for the two of them, for their household. It was sweet, really, that he would put so much time and energy into securing their future together. She did miss him, greatly, of course. And he did seem different lately, more distant. But in that moment – as she sat alone in her bed, with her entire world tucked neatly in the crook of her arm, exactly where he should be – she just couldn't seem to take her eyes of him. Little Christopher. His tiny fingers and his tiny eyelashes and his little itty-bitty nose that was smaller than her thumb nail...he took her breath away. It was distraction enough that she didn't really mind, or notice as much as she otherwise would have done, that her husband was never home, and that he paid very little interest in the life of his wife, or his new born son (or the two children who followed after that).

Elaine had met Robert unexpectedly outside of a café. She had been exiting the building one Sunday afternoon, with the golden sun still low in the sky. A book of poetry was tucked under her arm and she had a handbag on her shoulder. She remembered she was wearing a lemon-yellow sundress that her mother had made for her, with white high-heeled shoes and a white knee-length coat that had been a gift from her father. The air was crisp and clean, and her blonde curls flipped to one side as a gust of wind blew up the high street. As she stood for a moment, deciding which route to take back home, a gentleman in a suit came stomping up the pavement. He was completely oblivious to where he was going, entirely blinded by his own furious mood. The suit he wore was a deep burgundy, his shirt and tie both a gorgeous shade of royal blue. His face was twisted into a sour scowl.

He barged right into her, splashing a half a cup of coffee all over her, and Elaine watched her book and handbag topple to the floor – closely followed by herself, as her stilettoes twisted in the cracks of the pavement. She lost her balance.

"You stupid –!" the man had begun to say, as he turned sharply, his snarl ready to let go a barrage of verbal abuse. Elaine was grateful when his face softened upon looking at hers.

"Oh, I am awfully sorry," He said. His voice was soft and delicate and deep now. He extended a hand to her and helped her to her feet, "Are you okay?"

She was flustered, but otherwise everything appeared to be in order, "Yes, why thank you. I'm sorry, I didn't even see you!"

He leant down and picked up her belongings, "I'm Robert," he said.

"Elaine," she said.

It was only a small interaction. Elaine made sure not to hang around with strangers and did not believe in giving her contact details to anyone she did not know. So, she had simply said "Maybe I'll see you around?" and been on her merry way.

What was strange however was that the same man had shown up only a few days later at the front door of her home. Apparently, he had been invited there for dinner by her father. The four of them had sat and had a three-course dinner together, and Robert Brooker had certainly won her father's approval. Elaine wasn't entirely sure how it happened after that, but Robert had won her heart, and her hand, and the two were married within a year. Christopher was born less than a year after that.

Robert and Elaine had begun their relationship a romantic, deeply attached couple. They were highly respected and the neighbourhood highly approved of their marriage and the subsequent announcement of their pregnancy. Everyone always said they were "well-matched". But as time went on Elaine began to question what exactly they meant by this, as she realised that Robert and herself held very few similarities between the two of them. Of course, she loved him deeply, and didn't believe it possible to ever love another, but she did see a different side to Robert every now and again – a side to him that no one else appeared to ever see. It was the same side of him that had run into her that morning in front of the café. It was a dark and demanding side. One that she preferred to ignore, as best she could. It upset her to think that her husband could be so cruel.

A memory that tainted the birth of her son was the story of his conception. She had been asleep, in their marital bed one night, in the dark, and Robert had had a hard day at work. He had gotten home in a bad mood, eaten dinner in a bad mood, and had snapped at her all evening. After a long argument, she had given up trying to console him and make him feel better, and instead had gone up to bed, alone. He joined her some time later. He was not drunk – they did not keep alcohol in the house unless it was for a special occasion – and this was what made it all the more upsetting for her.

She had not looked up when the bedroom door opened. But she could see his shadow on the far wall as she squinted through her eyelashes. He stood tall and confident, as always. He was quiet. He stood there, looking at her, for just a few more seconds than Elaine found normal. The additional unexpected attention made her uneasy.

He came across the room and undid his tie. Robert did not appear to look away from her as he did so. He undid his shirt and his trousers, and, rather than hang them up and place them in the wardrobe like he normally did, he threw them onto the floor. To any other, this change in behaviour might have been overlooked, but Elaine felt a twinge in her gut that made her uneasy. Her heartbeat quickened and she prayed that he wasn't able to hear it, as she tightened her eyes, and clutched the duvet, and pretended to be asleep.

Through the darkness she felt the duvet and blankets lift

as he climbed into bed next to her. His warmth was suddenly very close, closer than she expected him to be, as he pressed himself against her back.

"Wake up," He said, a breathy whisper in her ear.

Elaine decided not to move. Instead, she lay very still.

His hands moved around her waist and rolled her onto her back. Her eyes flew open.

"Robert?"

"Shush."

He kissed her, forcefully, on the lips, and his hands cascaded down her nightdress and began to lift it up. She wriggled under his touch and tried to pull it back down again.

"Robert, please," she shook her head and tried to inch away from him in the bed, but his grip was tight. He pulled her back again, climbing on top of her and pinning her arms above her head.

"Robert!" She thrashed and pulled to try and get free. He took off her remaining clothes. But as she fought, his grip only tightened all the more, and his voice was less soft in her ear.

"Shut up." He said, "I've had a hard day, and you're my wife. Would you rather I found another woman for this?"

"No, of course not –"

"Why don't you want me to relax?"

"I do, I do want you to relax –" she assured him. She went to continue to say she just didn't want to do it in this way, and that her mindset simply was not in a romantic mood. But he cut her off.

"Good. Then stop fighting me. You always say you hate it when we fight. If you really loved me, you'd let me do this."

Elaine did not respond. Her brain was in shock and her thoughts were swirling around in her mind. What he said made perfect sense to her, and she agreed with it all, and of course she loved him, she loved him so much…and yet there was a part of her that wanted to fight back and rebel and tell him he was wrong for doing this to her when she didn't want to.

He forced himself upon her, and she lay on her back, her

knees towards the ceiling, and every muscle in her body incredibly tense. The experience was painful. She scrunched her eyes tightly shut and tried to think of other things. She tried to remember a time when Robert and her had been romantic with one another, a time when he had held her hand and walked with her, or been playful and made her laugh. In that moment, she could not bring such happy memories to the front of her mind. It felt like she was running, terrified, through a maze of her own thoughts, trying to escape what she was experiencing in that moment. This was not the Robert that she knew, the one she had fallen in love with...

He asked her if she was okay – just the once. She found herself quietly muttering "yes".

After, he climbed off and lay beside her. He huffed, irritable.

"What's wrong with you?"

"I'm sorry?" Elaine whispered, taken aback.

"You just lay there. You didn't do anything."

"I did say I didn't want to do it..." She heard her own voice and realised it was quiet, and timid. Her eyes looked anywhere but in his direction. She felt inexplicably sad, and echoingly hollow. Her sense of self felt smaller than a thimble.

To her further surprise, Robert laughed. One strong, unamused laugh, "Whatever," he said, "You were tighter. It felt way better than usual."

He pulled the duvet up over his shoulder and rolled away from her, so all she could see in the darkness was his bare back. She stared, blank and emotionless, at his silhouette.

The ceiling above them was decorated with swirling patterns, and Elaine found her eyes drawn up to them. They followed each curling line and each decorative fan in the plasterwork. The patterns then turned blurry, and she realised she had begun to cry.

God forbid he heard her. She shoved her face into her pillow and supressed the sobs that wanted to rock out of her shoulders. She breathed deeply and purposefully in an attempt to calm down.

What a hateful thing he had done.

She had closed her eyes and wished there was someone who would understand, someone who she could speak to. But she realised that if she was to retell the conversation they had had, that Robert perhaps hadn't done anything wrong. She *was* his wife. She *did* want him to relax. She *didn't* want him to find sexual release with another woman. She *did* love him...

She just didn't want to. Not tonight.

But she didn't tell him that. How was he to know? Her voice had been taken and supressed, the shock she was under had shaken her to her core in a way that made it impossible for her to speak of how she felt. He wasn't a mind-reader.

A few weeks after this, when Elaine had discovered she was pregnant, everybody was thrilled. Robert was delighted, as were Elaine's parents and all of their friends. Everyone congratulated them and spoke of the wonderful life that they would lead together as parents, as a family. They began giving her advice on pregnancy and birth and parenting. Her mother began sewing clothes for the infant before she was even three months pregnant, and people gave them gifts and cards that contained happy verses of the future and of how this little bundle of joy would be greeted into the world.

One afternoon, after being violently sick in the bathroom, Elaine sat in her nightdress and her robe in front of the dresser. She looked at her reflection and remembered how people said she was "glowing". In her eyes, she was just covered in sweat. Her breath smelled like the tuna sandwich she had for lunch, and her teeth were lined with the acidic taste of stomach bile.

In the mirror, she saw the reflection of the bed, behind her.

She looked down, with sad eyes, at her tiny bump. She placed a gentle hand on it and rubbed it through the silky nightdress.

How could a "bundle of joy" – something that everybody

was ever so deeply excited about – come from an evening that Elaine tried so desperately to forget?

Robert had awoken the morning after that awful night and had brought her breakfast in bed. He had made her a cup of tea, just the way she liked it, and read extracts of the newspaper to her. He had later that day gone to the local florist and brought home a huge bouquet of seasonal flowers – prominently daffodils, her favourite.

These actions only confused her more. She was so grateful for each thing he did – it felt like it was her birthday, the amount of love and attention he gave her, and the delicate way in which he would put an arm around her, or brush her hair away from her face, or gently kiss the tip of her nose. The flowers, too, and the food, were all such a wonderful surprise. And Elaine, outwardly, expressed love and affection for such acts of kindness. But somewhere, deep inside, she knew that all of these actions of his did not stem from love. No. They stemmed from guilt. They stemmed from fear. They stemmed from his desire to be seen by others as the best husband – the husband who cared so deeply for his wife, that he would put her needs before his own. And yes, that was what she had always wanted in a husband. But the way in which he was doing it did not sit right in her heart. It felt hollow and just for show. It felt like a façade, a parade. It felt like it was for the benefit of their friends and family and neighbours – not her.

Despite all this, she continued on. She was his wife. She was soon to be a mother. She was not going to be the lady who tore apart a family that, from the outside, appeared to be so perfect.

She rubbed her little bump and made a promise to the baby inside, whomever they were, that she would always take care of them. She would always put them first, she would always give them cuddles, and kiss it better, and smile at them when they approached her. She promised them that she would be the greatest mother she could possibly be.

And she promised them that if it ever came to a point

where she needed to protect that child from its own father – she would do it.

CHAPTER 10

Mickey found Marcus at his workplace. He had rung the business telephone number several times but apparently Marcus had always been busy. Mickey was getting worried that he was ignoring him.

Marcus had said he would come back later that afternoon to his flat – that day when the police had arrived. He hadn't. Mickey had then gone to work, returned from work, rang Marc to see if he was available – no answer.

Two days had now passed. And they were not any different to two regular days Mickey had spent at work in the past ten years or so. But they were the longest two days he had ever experienced – especially when all he wanted to do was talk to Marcus about everything. Especially when Marcus appeared to not want to talk.

The walk to the garage took about thirty minutes, normally. Even with his aging bones and stiff knees, today, Mickey managed it in just over fifteen.

He could see Marcus working on one of the cars as he approached – he had his blue overalls on, with the sleeves rolled up to the elbows, and his dark hair was slicked back on his head. The air was incredibly chill, and the bucket of soapy water that stood by his feet was steaming as the heat evaporated into the cold. He had a standard yellow sponge in his right hand and was scrubbing it across the car's number plate. Knowing Marcus, the car would be entirely spotless by the time he was finished with it.

"Oi!" Mickey called, when he was still some distance away.

He looked up from the car "Alrigh' Mouse?"

Mickey closed the distance between them in only a few paces, until he was stood on the opposite side of the car bonnet from him. There was only a second silence, but it was long enough for Marcus to know there was an issue, and to look up from the bonnet of his car.

Mickey sniffed. The air was cold; "You ignorin' me, or samffin'?" he asked. His tone was heavy, bold.

Marcus dropped the sponge into the bucket, and both pairs of eyes dropped briefly to watch the suds slap onto the concrete.

"Let's go somewhere a little less open."

"Why, you don't wanna be seen wiv me in public? Is that roight?"

"Mouse, it's not like that," Marcus lowered his voice, "I just want a chance to speak to you properly about all this."

Mickey took one more step forward. The toe of his leather boot nudged the bucket and more water sloshed about. There was approximately six inches or so between their faces. Mickey's face was not threatening or angry. His eyes squinted slightly as he fixed his unblinking stare onto Marcus. He placed a pointed finger under Marcus's chin, and used it to accentuate his words as he spoke:

"If you wanna speak to me, lad – you know where I fackin' live."

He took the scenic route home.

They had said nothing else after that, Mickey had been sure of it. Marcus had shouted his excuses and asked him to come back, but Mickey was not one to give in to grovelling. He shoved his hands deep into his pockets to protect them from the cold. His logic was this: if Marc really wanted the two of them to speak, then *he* would have to come to *him*.

What had irritated him more was the fact he had the audacity to use his nickname, when he had pretty much left him with no explanation in what was clearly an hour of need. *Mouse* was a nickname his school friends had given to him when he was little, when the Walt Disney cartoon had become most popular. In all honesty, it wasn't the most inventive of nicknames, but as a child he had found it inclusive – you knew you were in a solid group of friends if none of them went by their real names.

Mickey made a point of only allowing people he truly knew to call him Mouse. It was a matter of principle, in his book. If he didn't know them at all, it was Mickey. If they knew him slightly, it was often shortened to Mick. If it was in a doctor's office, or a letter to the council, or a utility bill, it was Michael. If it was a friend, or a family member, it was Mouse.

Marcus disappearing when Mickey felt it was, of all times, the most necessary for him to stick around, felt like a betrayal of sorts. Mickey did not like to associate with such people.

His feet thudded onto the pavement, his foul mood showing in every step. They took him through the park, towards the nicer end of town. It was a place he didn't often frequent, but a place he reckoned was home to a lot of his regulars at the theatre. The park, despite the cold, was full of life and lush grass, with hedgerows and beds filled with seasonal blooms. Above him in the trees, a pair of birds were chirping to one another. Mickey found himself amazed by how something as tiny as a robin, no more than three inches tall, could make such a loud and beautiful noise. He was sure his own voice would carry not nearly as well.

The path was golden-brown gravel and it crunched beneath his weight. He found a bench that overlooked the playing field, where he could see a young gentleman walking his dog. It was a sprightly thing – a springer spaniel, from what he could see – white and brown fur, and a playful lollop as it walked beside his owner. He carried a large stick in his mouth – clearly, the light of his life, in that moment. He looked to be one of the friendliest dogs Mickey had ever seen.

The seat was cold. Mickey could feel it even through his clothes. But he perched anyway, and leant back against the seat, where he lit a cigarette. He inhaled the smoke deep into his lungs and looked at the little stick between his fingers. As he breathed out, he felt truly appreciative of it. Just what he needed after a stressful week.

He didn't need Marcus. He knew that for certain. Mickey did not *need* anyone. He was a lone wolf and prided himself on being able to call himself such a thing and do so truthfully. He had met many people over the years who were phoney about who they were. He found it sad to see individuals so evidently lying about themselves, their personality, their abilities, their skills or their interests, just to please others. Mickey was not like that. He was upfront and honest, in all situations. Some people described him as blunt, or confrontational, or rude, or sometimes even odd. But this was not really the case. Mickey just stuck with what felt true to him, what felt good in his heart, according to his ways and his beliefs. Sure, it often prickled the backs of others who disagreed with him – and Mickey had gotten into a fair few arguments and fights over many a thing, both trivial and serious topics – but Mickey had found it was the greatest way to walk through life with the highest level of clarity. Sure, Mickey had a great many enemies due to his straight-talking. But it was no more than anyone else had. It was just he could clearly see his enemies, as they weren't disguised as friends who were pretending to like him.

How much easier would life be if two people who didn't like one another just said it aloud and be done with it. No time wasted, two individuals who can then go in their separate ways rather than waste time and energy and breath on saying "how do you do? How is work? How is your wife?" When, in reality, one does not care how the other is, does not remember what they do for a living, and thinks their wife is the most hateful, ugly woman that has ever existed? To Mickey, it just felt like wasted energy. And, as he was now past his fiftieth year, he did not feel he had the energy to make polite chit-chat with people he didn't like. Apart from at work, of course, where it was in the job description to always be polite to the guests.

That was why, upon betrayal, Mickey wasted no time either in making it clear to Marcus that he would not be spending any more energy on him and their friendship – and also made it clear that if Marcus should wish to speak with him again, then Mickey would not be the one to begin the conversation. As far as he was concerned, it was a closed door, an unopened book – or any other metaphor he wanted to use. He was done with it. He'd dropped him. Goodbye.

He leant forward, resting his elbows on his knees, and tapped his cigarette so the ash fell onto the gravel below. Down the path, he could see a young blonde lady walking with her three children. One was tiny and was being pushed in a push chair. The other two walked, ever so well-behaved, by their mother's side, holding hands. The eldest pointed into the tree where the robin was still singing his little heart out.

"Mum, look!" He said, "a bird!"

The mother turned her head to see where her son was pointing. She smiled and acknowledged his discovery with a comment about the bird and how handsome he was, and how brave he must be to be sat all the way up in that tree, so tall.

She was blonde, and her curls cascaded down onto her black winter coat. They were all dressed in black – she, a black dress, and the young ones all in very smart coats and trousers and skirts. The eldest could not have been any older than six, with the middle child being about three years old or so – the both of them had blonde hair, just like their mother. The little one in the pushchair had dark hair and couldn't have been more than a year old. His eyelids were bobbing up and down, threatening to close for a nap.

Mickey caught their eye as they passed.

"Robins roost together, y'know," He said to the boy, "there are some roosts that can have as many as two hundred thousand robins in 'um."

"Wow!" The boy said, "That's a lot of robins!" He looked up at his mum again, "Did you hear that, mummy? Two hundred...*thousands*!" The child stumbled over such a big number, having probably never heard it before.

"Yes, it's lovely isn't it?" she said. She smiled at Mickey and he gave her a kind smile back, "Come along now, children. Don't disturb this good gentleman."

She ushered them away. Her smile was kind, and it reached her eyes. She seemed to truly be enjoying being out of the house with her young ones. Mickey didn't blame her, considering they were the best-behaved children Mickey had ever come across. Just before they were more than an arm's length away, Mickey said: "I'm sorry for your loss, love."

He said it sincerely, quietly. Her eyes met his and she nodded, grateful.

"I won't bore you. You've probably heard enough of people's sympathies and the like."

She nodded again, her face fighting between a smile and a deep sadness. The smile won, as it did, every time, "Thank you." She said. Her eyes bore deeply into his.

"No worries. See you around, Elaine."

"And you, Mouse."

CHAPTER 11

Marcus had been spending more and more time at Jane's house lately. Any spare moment he had, he spent it with her. He was, to say the least, a little obsessed.

She didn't mind him being there as often as he was. And what surprised him most was that he didn't mind working around her crazy schedule. She wanted to meet for breakfast at 8AM? He was not only there on time – he was there *early*. She wanted to go to the cinema? He was looking up the films schedule, booking the tickets, putting aside money to buy her popcorn and pick 'n' mix sweets. All before she'd even had chance to finish the thought.

He had never before been this *interested*. No one had ever managed to get him out of bed before eight o'clock in the morning. Not even an emergency alarm could get him up that early. He'd snooze the fire alarm for another ten minutes before he'd evacuate his bed.

But not with Jane.

He awoke that morning wrapped in her arms and her hair and her bedsheets. The heavenly scent of her skin was all around him. He held in his mind the memories of the night before, thinking they could more than likely be a dream. He was delighted when he opened his eyes to find her there, draped across him. Her breathing was soft and delicate on his neck.

Being careful not to move himself and disturb her, he

looked across at the bedside table and the alarm clock that rested upon it. Four-twenty-three. The two dots in the centre of the numbers flashed and lit up the dark room like an electronic heartbeat.

It being late winter, the sun would not be rising for at least another three hours. He felt startlingly awake, despite wanting nothing more than to slip back into the restful cocoon of sleep. He caressed Jane's hair through his fingertips. It felt like silk. He sniffed it. She smelled like raspberries and lemon zest. A sweet, subtle, citrusy scent. He found it calming, as his mind threatened to teeter into less relaxing topics. Despite his fighting, the curiosity of it won him over.

Marcus had found it unsettling when the police officers had come knocking at Mouse's door. In the moment, he had promised Mouse everything. He had wanted to stay and defend him, stick up for him, tell the officers it was all untrue. However, when the door had been closed in his face, Marc had felt especially isolated. Mickey had not even said goodbye.

Marcus tried to imagine how he himself would feel in that situation. What could have made Mickey so anxious and erratic and quick to be rid of him? Marc had never seen his friend act in such a way. Mouse was, despite the nickname, the most confident, least-shy, most-brash individual Marcus had ever met. Nothing quietened him. Nobody told him what to do. Nobody stood up to him and told him he was wrong. Mouse was strong, fearless, brave...

Did he have the potential to be a murderer?

Marc's eyes stared into the darkness as the thoughts raced in his mind. The room was blanketed in a blue-grey filter. The outline of a desk, a chair, a wardrobe, a set of drawers, could all be seen. Jane's room was like a page from a glossy catalogue. Everything was white or a pale shade of grey and accented in copper. Every object had a rightful place, and Jane had a way of making sure everything always returned to it if it had been used. Marcus was amazed that the only thing found on the floor were his own clothes, where he had discarded them the night before. Even then, he knew that if Jane woke up before he did the next morning, that he would turn to find his boxer shorts neatly folded, atop his other clothes. They would all be piled in the order that he would need them to put them on again. And that they wouldn't be on the floor – oh, no. Nothing was on the floor, except a beautifully soft, perfectly white rug.

Jane would never be able to kill anybody – he could tell. And that was without having to get to know her any better than he already did. Some people, you could just tell, straight up. For most, he presumed, it was a no. Delilah, the old lady who owned the corner shop? She wouldn't do it. Mr Bradshaw, Marc's next-door neighbour, the history teacher at the school – who spoke every day to a class of thirty teenagers about wars and murders and brutality – no, he wouldn't do it. Even the hobo that begged for change outside the local chippy – he wouldn't do it either, not even if Marc offered him a free bottle of vodka in return.

But Mouse...?

Mouse was kind-hearted, strong, reassuring, and out-going. He was the life of the party. A brilliant storyteller. A man who could put even the most erratically anxious of people into a calming state with just a good cup of tea and a short conversation. But it was this spellbinding confidence that made Marcus ponder. Marcus had witnessed the faith that people placed in Mouse. What were his capabilities?

Marcus peeled himself from under Jane's sweeping arms, and she sighed softly in her sleep. She rolled over, away from him; her gorgeous hair spilling across the pillow like a river. He took a long moment to look at her again. *God...she was gorgeous.*

His feet swung over the bed and he got up and pulled his boxers from the disarray that he had left the night before. He put them on and quickly folded the rest of his clothes and placed them on top of his shoes, on the floor. He didn't know why, but he felt a little bit proud of himself – knowing that, when she awoke in the morning, Jane would see and appreciate his child-like effort to copy her.

He stood and walked across the soft rug, feeling the fibres, chilly, between each of his toes. He walked across to the window and pulled back the pale grey, floor-length, Ikea curtains, and peeked through the white blinds that hung behind them.

The street on which Jane lived was a crowded one – terraced houses, with cars squeezed in, nose to tail. They went all the way along, more than one per house. The remaining road was only questionably wide enough to actually drive down it. The streetlamps lit the road with a deep orange glow. Dark shadows of tall fruit trees stretching out down the sloping tarmac.

Marcus liked the night. He would always rather be awake during the darkest hours, rather than the daytime, simply because it was quieter. He enjoyed listening to the few people who were also awake. A TV blared somewhere in the adjoining house. One of Jane's housemates shuffled about in slippers downstairs. A grey and white cat roamed along a garden wall, stretching its back out as it did so, gingerly. A lone girl in an apron and a hood pulled tightly around her face against the cold, walked quickly up the pavement, hurrying home from her shift in a local pub.

Marcus looked up at the night's sky – a deep blue, with not a single star.

Tomorrow, he vowed, he would speak to Mouse, and find out what was going on.

CHAPTER 12

Elaine stared out of the kitchen window.

The day was crisp and cold outside. The grass was blanketed in a thin layer of frost – possibly one of the last frosts of the year, until the winter came again. With the sun rising over the houses in the distance, the new-found heat caused the frost to rise into vapour and dissipate into the day. Elaine sighed, heavily. She found herself wondering if she, too, could follow the same pattern in nature and disappear. Each day had made her limbs feel heavy and her eyes protest about being open. She struggled each morning to even get out of bed, and to dress herself, and to stand in front of her three children and smile and laugh and play and come up with creative and positive ideas for them to do as a family. The evenings made her feel scared. Constricted and anxious and fidgety – she would pick at her fingernails and chew on her bottom lip and fiddle with her blonde curls. She would pace, and pather, and her mind would race. The hands of the clock on the mantel piece just ticked away, inconsiderately. She had found herself every night since it had happened still awake, downstairs, in the living room or kitchen, staring out of the window into the garden, until well-past three in the morning.

Her eyes were drawn over and over again to the place where he had lay.

The grass was still stained with the blood that had oozed

from under his helmet. Now a horrid black which contrasted so starkly with the white frost and the lush green grass. Amidst the flower beds and the apple tree and the children's playthings, it was a dark and horrid spot that one could not help but be drawn to. It sucked the life and the playfulness and the joy out of an otherwise colourful and beautiful garden. They had hosted barbeques in that garden, together. They had talked with the neighbours over the wall, and exchanged Christmas presents one year over it. For Christopher, it was the place where he had taken his first steps. It was the place they had had snowball fights and made snow angels. The garden in which they had raked up the leaves together in autumn, and planted daffodil bulbs in the spring, and mowed the grass and picked fresh flowers to display on the dining table. Robert had made a picnic for the two of them one year, for their anniversary, and had lit candles all the way down the stone path. The garden had looked so contained and beautiful and held so many memories, so much life.

And now, after one night, all those memories were tainted with one vision, one awful early morning, followed by one awfully long week.

She held a teacup up to her lips, surprised by how steady her hands were. Another heavy sigh escaped through her lips, and she blew it across the hot tea to cool it. It reminded her of the feeling of blowing out birthday cake candles.

All her birthdays would be without Robert, from now on.

An awful memory crept into her mind. A birthday only two years before, when Elaine had wanted to go into town dress-shopping with a friend of hers. She had needed Robert to take her in the car and drop her off in the centre of town. Robert had gotten angry that Elaine wasn't spending the day with him. He'd refused to take her. She had been upset, but instead figured that they would spend the day together. But no. Instead, he spent the entire day in his office, reading. When she went to ask him if he wanted to go out for dinner, or to watch the television set with the children for the evening, he had snapped at her to get out, to leave him alone.

"You didn't want to spend the day with me, Elaine – so I'm only giving you what you asked for! You made this happen!"

He had then slammed the door in her face.

What an awful birthday that had been. She had ended up hiding in the bathroom, so that the children didn't see her tears, and sobbing into a bath towel to muffle the sound. She knew that if he saw her upset, he would only get all the more annoyed with her and her "womanly ways". Her "emotional stupidity". It had happened too many times before, so she knew what to expect from him.

"Why are you crying?! God, there's nothing that makes you happy, is there? You're useless! You're so ungrateful! What's the matter with you?!"

His words cut deep and made her feel guilty for the way she felt. He had been awful to her, but she had no courage to stand up to him and tell him he was wrong, because the seed of doubt that he had planted, all too long before, was now deep-rooted and refused to decay. Whenever she thought about telling him how awful he could be to her, she knew that he would only respond by naming all the good things he had ever done for her. How ungrateful she was, he would say. How the work he did was for her, and that the work gave him stress, and the stress caused this anger – so, really, the reason he was stressed was because he provided for her. She felt guilty about everything, and always knew that if he was in a bad mood that it would be her fault. She found herself trying her best to usher him away from situations that could potentially cause upset. She ensured he never lost anything – she always knew where everything was. She always made sure dinner was ready for him when he got home – therefore there could be no complaining that dinner was not ready when he was so hungry from working all day. Every argument they had ever had, she did her absolute best to try and avoid it ever happening again. But there was always something she missed, always a job she had forgotten, or a spot on the carpet she hadn't cleaned well enough.

Elaine sipped from the teacup again.

She had gotten very close, once.

There was one evening when he came home drunk. Apparently, there had been a bad deal at work, and the men from the office had all gone to the pub around the corner for a casual drink to make one another feel better. Robert was in a foul mood that evening. He got home and could hardly stay awake at the dinner table. As a lady with proper table manners, Elaine was mortified, and told the children not to laugh when their father lay his head down on the table and got his tie in their beef casserole. She told them that their father was poorly and should go to bed. Robert had gotten angry at the laughter, and at being told what to do. He had stood up from his seat on the table and turned his attention to their middle child. Little Lucy. She was so small, only three years old. He had told her to stop laughing. She had gone very quiet and scared and had started to cry, and then he had taken out his belt and Elaine had begged him to stop. The only time she had ever had the courage to raise her voice at him.

"*Not* the children." She had said, confidently. Her voice was like ice. Her eyes stared at him, echoing with thunder and lightning from her fury, "Take your hands *off* her."

Robert had held her gaze for a long moment. He seemed surprised by the new-found confidence, despite the years of his repeatedly beating her down mentally. With a level of unnecessary flair, he took his hands off her daughter.

Elaine had ushered the three children into the other room and had handed baby Tommy to their eldest, Christopher, to carry. She encouraged them to go and play upstairs. Timid, they did so. She had closed the kitchen door behind them.

"You're ever so confident, aren't you?" He said. He smiled, but his eyes were dark and empty.

"Don't you *ever* bring the children into this, Robert," she said. Her hands shook, but she remained firm, "You can say and do what you want to me; but you don't ever lay a hand on our children when you're in one of these moods. Do you understand? *Ever.*"

He placed both of his palms onto the kitchen table, stooping over, and looked up at her. His slicked-back hair was dishevelled and his smile wicked and cunning. He was thinking. Oh, how she hated it when he looked at her that way. It made her stomach flip and her toes feel numb.

And then, just like that, he snapped.

He slammed the table, smashing one of the plates that lay within arm's reach of him, and then grabbed the table from its legs. With an almighty noise, similar to the snarl of an animal, he heaved and flipped the table over, to the left – plates and knives and forks and beef casserole flying all over the kitchen.

He took three fast paces and all of a sudden he had gone from being the opposite side of the room, the opposite side of the table, to being centimetres away from her face, clutching her jaw in just one of his strong hands and hissing at her through his teeth.

"You *dare* tell me what to do, in my own house? With my own children?" Spit flew from between his teeth and splattered onto her face and she grimaced, her eyes screwed tight. She tried to turn her face away from his, but he held her fast, until it hurt, and until his nails dug into the skin, "You disgust me." He said, "Of all the things I've done for you, all the things I give for you – this house, those clothes – and you have the audacity to tell me what to do?" He shook his head, and his voice softened, as if like magic, "You should know better than that...look now, look what you made me do...look at all this mess...such a pity. It looked such a good meal." He sighed and smiled a kind smile at her, a smile that made her feel queasy. The grip he held on her face lessened slightly, but he did not remove his hand, "Thankfully, as you said, I'm not feeling too well, so no matter – no need to cook anything new. No need to worry, okay? Everything's fine. Everything's okay. I'm sorry, I didn't mean to yell, you know I don't like it when I have to yell at you."

He went to kiss her, but she moved her head again slightly.

"Kiss me, Elaine. Please." His eyes darkened over again, "I've apologised for the yelling."

She allowed him to kiss her on the lips, but her face remained still and lifeless. She was proud of herself for not crying. She wouldn't allow him the satisfaction.

He turned away and corrected the position of the table.

"There we are," he said, "good as new." Robert stood and straightened his tie. He used a tea-towel to wipe off the gravy, as best he could, "I'm off to change and go to bed darling, my head does hurt something awful. Clean this up, please?"

He waited for her to nod. She did. He smiled at her, again, a kind smile, and left the room.

It was in that moment, after that incident, as she stared at her messy kitchen, caused by her reckless and unpredictable husband, that she had the thought. She swept up the jagged shards of plate and mopped up the gravy. She folded the tablecloth and put it to be washed and laid out a fresh one. She picked up the flowers that had remained mostly intact, despite being thrown from the vase in the ruckus, and surrounded by shattered glass where they lay on the floor.

She looked at the destruction and thought of the mess that had taken her hours to clean up, after putting the children to bed.

It felt as if her skin was made of porcelain. And that with everything that Robert did to upset her, it disrupted the peace that she so desperately tried to create in her suburbia, the family life that she so longed for. Each time he spat at her, a crack formed around her smile, around her eyes, on the skin of her arms or hands. Just a small crack here, a little chip there. But bit by bit, he was breaking her. She was cracking. She was losing her patience.

It was that evening, in the dark, with her hands cut from the broken crockery, and her dress splattered with gravy, that she first had the idea.

Perhaps, she thought, it wouldn't be so disastrous if her husband was to die.

It was a seed that planted itself next to the previous one in her brain, and with each time after that moment that Robert cracked her, the seed rooted itself all the more deeply into her mind.

Perhaps, Elaine thought, she could kill him.

CHAPTER 13

A few weeks earlier...

F elix sat down at the bar.
      "Double whisky."
      "Ice, sir?"
"No."

The bar was by no means empty, but the place had a calmed and quiet atmosphere to it that evening. Everyone was speaking in hushed tones, or sat quietly, alone, with their drink – like Felix did. Even the two gents at the pool table in the corner were not raucous or loud with their game. The colourful balls tapped one another quietly – the sound was almost relaxing to listen to. Unlike on your average Friday night the juke-box was turned down low. The tunes were almost too quiet to make out the song that was playing, aside from perhaps the bass beat and a few very clear lyrics. Felix guessed it was something by Gene Pitney playing presently, due to the deep tones of the gent's voice that was singing – but he cared too little to explore the thought further, or to check.

Felix threw down a handful of coins that made out the price of the drink to the penny. He looked up at the bartender only briefly. His face was not friendly.

He rested his forearms on the soft, worn-away wood of the bar. Soft due to the amount of years that damp cloths and beer had been rubbed over it. The wood was as splinter-free as you could get it. Felix picked up a card beermat from the square plastic container that was stacked with hundreds of them and placed his drink on top of it. He was a carefree fellow, but he was not careless.

Felix sat and looked about himself from the padded bar stool on which he sat. The place was filled with the deep brown tones of dark wood, layers upon layers upon layers of varnish from over the years. The seats were made of sad, cracking leather, that, he guessed, had never been cleaned. The bar stools were covered with a deep forest green cloth that felt like velvet. The walls were decorated with as many picture frames as would fit – all black and white, of people and places and farm animals that nobody would be able to recognise. Faces that had definitely existed, but had gotten lost in time, faded from memory, with not a single living soul who now knew their name. Felix believed that the point of life was to be remembered. He was making sure that, if ever his picture was placed upon a wall he would never be merely glanced over. He would not be looked at as a ghost with nothing interesting to say. He would be remembered for the deeds he did, for the things he said, for the places he went, for the ladies he slept with. Being remembered didn't have to mean for doing something good – what was the difference between good and bad anyway? It was all a matter of perspective. He had read once that there was an African tribe or something where a man's rite of passage was to have a very sharp stick pierced through his penis, and that if the man should cry then he isn't a real man after all. Felix knew that if anybody tried to jam a stick through his manhood then he'd knock them out, or something worse – and people would not think him bad for it. Culture and society meant different things. It depended on whom people were, what they believed in, where they lived. He did not bother to worry himself over what was right and what was wrong in the eyes of others – he was simply living his life as he believed he should do. He judged situations using his own basis of right and wrong. Good and bad were not black and white – it was all very similar shades of grey. Just like in the old photographs, in fact – all grey. Not black and white. That's how everything, ever, would be remembered. After all – nobody got famous by asking for permission.

The door had two entry ways. One around to the front, through a big wooden Tudor-looking door with an old-fashioned latch and a circular ring-like door handle. The one towards the back was more like somebody had gotten their old kitchen door, painted it an unflattering shade of green, then stuck it on and pretended it worked. It had a window through it. Felix looked over, and the back of a figure's head caught his eye – somebody stood just outside, under the porch awning, smoking a cigarette.

Ah, so his companion was here at last.

"Get me another whisky." Felix said to the bartender, as the man walked in through the horrid green door.

He had a black fleece jacket wrapped round his slender frame – a coat that was, by any means, too baggy, but it seemed to suit his demeanour. He walked with a bit of a swagger; his shoulders pulled back, and his head stooped low. He eyed up the small crowd in the pub. His hands were dug deep into his pockets. Out of sight, he flicked the lid of his lighter on and off.

"Alrigh' Felix?" He said, sitting down next to him.

He settled himself on the neighbouring stool and browsed the many bottles of liquor and draught pumps that were displayed in the golden-yellow bulb light. The bartender placed Felix's order down in front of him, and they did the usual exchange of monies. Felix placed a beermat underneath it, then slid it across the soft wood until it was underneath where his companion sat.

"Drink up," Felix said.

He took a sniff, "Yer don't 'alf drink some fackin' shit, you do."

"When in Rome."

They clinked glasses and both took a sip. Felix allowed the burn of the alcohol to fill his mouth and make his gums and tongue tingle. The taste that remained was sweet, honey tones, mixed with a gorgeous warm smoke. He sat up a little taller.

"What the fack is that?"

"Whisky," Felix answered.

"C'mon then, why did you drag me 'ere?"

"I think you know."

"Oh?"

Felix took another sip. The room still had a brilliant air to it. Calming quietness, with the juke box now whirring as it flipped to another track. Felix leant down low over the bar and his voice hushed all the more.

"You heard of Robert Brooker?" He asked.

The man raised an eyebrow, "Depends on who's askin'."

"He's got me a job. Offerin' a lot for it."

"Not interested."

"Mouse, I'm not kiddin' when I say it's a *lot*."

Mickey shook his head and put the foul whisky down on the bar. His posture stiffened and he zipped up his fleece jacket, so it was right underneath his chin.

"I don't fackin' care 'ow much you say it is, I'm not interested. I don't do that kinda shit."

"Mouse, it's an easy job, you'll walk it, mate."

"Yeah, walk right back into prison again, won't I?" He met his eyes and stared at him, aggressive, "You just wanted me as your fall guy, din' ya? In case everything goes wrong and you want someone easy to chuck under the bus."

"Mouse –"

"Don't *fackin'* call me that, yer bastard."

"Mick, please – it's easy. He wants some prissy little blonde sortin' out. She's causing him trouble, is all. She's nothin'. Nobody would miss her. She's in the house on her own, more often than not. She doesn't have a job, doesn't have friends – nobody would notice."

Mickey shook his head, "No."

"I thought we were brothers?"

"Yeah. We are. But every time I try and do samthin' noice

for you, you go and throw it back in ma fackin' face. Yer only out to use me, you are. You're a fackin' miserable excuse for a human bein'. I ain't about that life anymore, Felix. I ain't into it. Stop tryna force me down yer twisted road." He got up from the stool and pushed the whisky back across the bar towards Felix, "You can keep yer fackin' devil's piss as well."

"Mick! Come back!"

"Fack off, yer no-good back-stabbin' bastard."

And with that, Mouse was gone.

CHAPTER 14

Elaine had lay awake that night, after the table and beef casserole incident, staring at the ceiling.

Robert lay beside her, snoring softly, his arms resting over his chest, rising and falling with every breath he took.

She kept fighting the thought, but it kept clawing its way back in again.

She couldn't...could she?

Her fingers fidgeted and she picked at her nails.

He was awful, but he wasn't that awful...was he? He didn't deserve to *die* from what he'd done...

No, no, she was being silly...of course she couldn't do it...

The clock on the wall ticked away the seconds. Ticked... ticked...ticked...

She looked over at him and his placid face, his open mouth, his nostrils that flared every now and again as he breathed. His skin was slack and relaxed, his brow not frowning, for once. He looked ever so peaceful. She imagined him laying like that, dressed in his finest suit, contained in a silk-lined wooden box...

Gosh, what was she *thinking?!*

They had children together – he was a *father*. The father of *her own* children. She couldn't take away their only father figure. She couldn't do that to them.

But then again...

The image flashed in her mind of their timid daughter, the tears streaming down her cheeks as she stood in front of her daddy and wriggled to get away from him. She remembered the horrid look he had on his face when he looked at the three little ones. He had not looked like a father, but instead he had looked like a man drunk on power as well as bourbon. He looked like a man who was sadistic and cruel – a man who was willing to use a woman's children against her in order to get what he wanted from her, in order to control her. And those children that he was so willing to use, like pieces in a chess game, were *his own* children.

Elaine looked over at him again and scowled at his face through the darkness.

It felt like she was sleeping next to a giant wild cat. Peaceful if undisturbed, but unpredictable and ferocious if poked with a stick. She knew that, if she was to do it, she would have to pick her timing correctly. If she misjudged herself, even for a second, even for a moment, or changed her mind at any point and couldn't go through with it, he would roar and break free from any trap she could set for him, and turn against her, one last time. She knew that if the boot was on the opposite foot, he would not hesitate. Not for a second. Not if he was blinded by his own rage. He would kill *her* without a second thought. It was only a matter of time, really. One day she would not be pretty enough, not be smiling enough, and their children will have grown up and moved out to safety, so she wouldn't be needed to care for them. What then? Would he keep her around? Would he want an aging, wrinkly, older woman sucking his resources dry? Or would he scout about for a younger model? Elaine guessed, very strongly, it would be the latter.

He did not love her. He never had – she was sure. She was just a trophy to him. He wanted the prettiest, loveliest, most well-behaved wife, and he had made sure that was what he had. But in twenty years, she would no longer fit the bill.

He would either divorce her and leave her nothing, or he would dispose of her in another way.

He would get rid of her, make her disappear into the night, make it look like she abandoned her own family, make himself out to be the victim. And then he would live the story of the man who found the perfect, younger, lovelier lady to look after him into his older years. That was the way it would go. His reputation was everything. It all played out in her mind. Her eyes were open, but they did not see the dark room, or the bed – they saw his face, his laughter, him coming at her with a knife or a hammer or his own bare hands, whatever he saw fit.

She grabbed the corner of her pillow.

Could she?

She lifted it and held it in front of her. She looked at him again, sleeping. He snorted, and breathed a stuttery, dry breath in, before the rhythm of his lungs calmed down again. What if she was to stop that rhythm? Was she strong enough? Could she hold that pillow down over his face, and do so long enough and firm enough until he stopped breathing? Could she fight against him when his limbs inevitably lashed out and tried to tackle her off from on top of him?

Elaine clutched the pillow, frozen. Her mind played out all the possible scenarios in her head. *What if* this, *what if* that... she could see more instances where he would throw her off and return the act – and do so until the bitter end.

Amazingly, the thought of him killing her did not fill her with as much fear as she thought it would, initially. What filled her with fear about the idea of being suffocated was not that her life would be lost, but that the lives of her three children would then be ruled by their father. He would be alone in the house with them all the time, with nobody else around to take the blows and the anger. Nobody would be around to protect them from his fury and his bad moods and his stress. It would not be her life that was taken if he was to do it, but the lives of Christopher, Lucy and Tommy would also be ruined.

She huffed. What an awful situation.

Hugging the pillow close to her chest, Elaine leant forward over it, as if she was giving it a hug. It had been so long since she had been held – properly, that is, delicately, romantically, reassuringly.

She felt so alone, so confused by her own thoughts. The darkness clouded around her, like her visions did in her mind. Was she a bad person, for thinking these things? What she an awful mother, for wanting to take away the father of her children? Was she evil for even thinking of taking her pillow and pressing it over her husband's face, and pressing and pressing and pressing down until his lungs no longer naturally wanted to draw in breath? Was she evil for wanting to take that decision into her own hands, to protect herself and her family from the inevitable – even if the threat to them was not imminent?

Her stomach turned with guilt. Her mind raced with fear. Her hands shook with the confusion of it all.

She wished there was someone who she could talk to. She wished there was someone who understood, someone who could just listen, just understand – someone who could take away the isolation of it all. Someone she could confide in, just so that, if something happened, she knew that there was somebody else to look out for her little ones. She wanted a person to help, to listen. She wanted a friend.

The clock continued to tick, the time continued to pass, and with each passing moment Elaine became more aware of how alone she was, of how scared she was, of how trapped she felt.

She placed her pillow back on top of the mattress, where she had picked it up from, and lay down. She turned her back on Robert, and looked towards the window, and the moonlight that seeped from behind the curtains.

Elaine closed her eyes and tried her hardest to fall back to sleep.

But all that fell were tears.

CHAPTER 15

Marcus stood outside Mickey's flat. He rapped his knuckles against the wood again. This was the fourth time he had tried.

Each time when there was no answer, he told himself this was the last time he would knock. And each time he went to lower his hand, he found himself pausing, convincing himself he needed to knock louder, and trying again.

It was raining outside today. His black jacket was soaked, as was his hair, his shoes –all of him, really. Jane had offered him an umbrella that morning when he had apologised and insisted he needed to dash off. She was amazed by the breakfast he had made for her to eat in bed. He had kissed her delicately on the lips, the nose, the forehead, apologised again, said he would explain in full at a later date, and then rushed off into the morning.

And here he was, stood alone, in the corridor, outside of Mickey's flat, and he was getting no answer.

Marc was beginning to get irritated. He proceeded to whack a flattened palm against the door, rather than just his knuckles:

BANG-BANG-BANG-BANG-BANG-

"Alrigh', alrigh', don't take it off the hinges, will ya?"

Marcus spun round. Here he was, keys in hand, stern gaze in his eyes as he stood, just a few paces behind Marcus.

"Where've you been?" Marc asked.

"I could say the same to you, kiddo." He unlocked the door, "You comin' in for a brew, or what?"

They didn't say anything as Mickey held the door open and Marc walked through. He assessed the look of the apartment. It looked tidier than usual. The tiny flat had been dusted and vacuumed and every piece of fabric had been straightened. Every surface was wiped down, everything in the kitchenette was off the counters, tucked neatly away into the cupboards. Even yesterday's newspaper was neatly folded, atop the coffee table.

"Not like you to be up this early." Mouse said, putting the kettle on. Neither of the men took off their jackets.

"I wanted to see you."

"Still – there must be a reason. Nathin' ever got you up before midday, 'cept that girl." He pulled the mugs from the cupboard and spooned the sugar carefully into each one, "Still seein' 'er?"

"Yeah, I am," Marcus nodded. He couldn't help but smile, but tried to hide it, "We're doing great, really."

"Good."

The apartment was incredibly still. Neither of them had sat down, neither of them spoke for a long minute. Mickey poured the hot water over the tea bags and gave them a stir. The only sound for some time was the tinkle of the spoon as it hit the circular edge of the ceramic.

Marcus watched Mickey's face. He looked tired, aged somewhat. Marc couldn't tell whether it was how his friend had always looked, or if a few rough night's sleep had taken their toll. In all honesty, he had never really noticed that Mickey had aged at all. It was a process that had occurred so slowly since they had met, so minorly, that each passing day held no difference to the one before it. However now Marcus remembered the first day they had met. Several years ago, Marcus had been just a child, and thought of how the creases around Mickey's eyes and cheeks were now deeper and more defined than they used to be. He had bags under his eyes – from lack of sleep? Or just from the passing of time?

Mouse reached into the tiny fridge and pulled out a glass bottle of milk. He tipped a drop or two into each of the mugs before placing it back.

He looked at the way Mickey walked about his kitchen – not the tallest of men, but a man whose reputation made him appear larger than he was. He had slender limbs that held more strength than could be seen on the surface, and a face that, when resting, was neither happy nor sad, but rather thoughtful and perhaps somewhat serious. He stooped slightly whenever he stood. Not so much that it would be noticeable, unless Mickey was to stand up tall. He was a man whom time had been mostly kind to – he was once, and still was, to some extent, handsome. But was he a man whom *life* had been kind to? Was he able to do the thing that Marcus had convinced his brain he had done? There was only one way to find out.

"I did come here for a reason, Mouse," Marcus said. He stood on the opposite side of the kitchenette counter, opposite where Mouse stood, making the tea for them both.

"I thought you 'ad." The teabags were fished out of the hot water with the spoon. Mickey gave them a good pinch with his fingers before flinging them across the kitchen, where they landed expertly in the bin – clearly a skill he had mastered over the years. Several cups of tea, several times of day. Marcus thought how it was very rare for Mickey to be seen without a mug in his hand.

Marc found himself hesitating, but he forced himself to push on: "I'm gonna ask it bluntly," he warned, "Did you do it?"

Mickey turned and placed the mugs on the counter. He slid one closer to Marcus. "Do what?"

"You know what."

"If I fackin' knew d'you think I'd be fackin' askin' ya?"

The two held eye contact for a few seconds. Marcus was still unsure whether or not to believe him: "The man – Robert Brooker – did you kill him?"

The question hung in the air, suspended between the two

of them as if it were floating in water and neither of them could believe what they were seeing. It left Marcus's lips with a casual, rather than accusing tone – as if Marc had instead asked whether he'd watched the football match that weekend, rather than ask if he'd shot a man dead in his own back garden.

"What kind of a question is that?"

"A blunt one."

"You accusin' me of killin' sam fackin' bloke I never even 'eard of before?"

"No," Marcus clarified, sternly, "I'm asking you if you did it. There's no accusation." He sipped his tea.

Mickey lowered his voice. His face looked disappointed: "You really think I did it?"

Marcus took a deep breath. His dark eyebrows knitted into a deep frown, "I've thought about it," Marc answered slowly, choosing his words carefully, "and I think it's something you'd be capable of, if you ever decided to."

"Well, yeah, I'm able to. *More* than able to. But why would I wanna pop the clogs of some geezer I ain't even connected to?"

"Why did the police come to question you then, if you don't have any affiliation with him?"

"Who are you, some undercover copper or samfin'?"

Marcus laughed, a genuine laugh, "No, I'm your friend. And I'm someone you can trust, in all instances, should you need to, not just–" he moved his hands about "–this, now."

Mickey smiled, "Thanks, kid."

"You still haven't answered my question."

Mouse's eyes looked across at him. He took a sip of tea, "The old bill seem to think I have samfin' to do wiv it. I was seen wiv 'im on the evenin' he's thought to have died, chasin' his car down the street."

Marcus drew back, "You were chasing him?"

"Nah, nah, it ain't like that." Mouse answered, shaking his head like he'd just been asked a stupid question by a child, "He dropped his fackin' wallet din' he? It had a fair few paper ones in there, so I didn't wanna let him leave without it."

"So, you chased him down? You spoke to him?"

"Yeah, of sorts. He talked at me. I listened. He's a fackin' cunt – wish I'd kept his bleedin' wallet in the end."

Marcus snorted a laugh into his mug as he took another sip. The tea was hot, sweet and good. It warmed his hands and his heart. Mouse made an excellent brew. In fact, it was Mouse who had made him his first cup of tea, back when he was still a child. Mouse had insisted that there was nothing that a good cup of tea couldn't fix. Cold weather, a broken heart, shock, a shit day – tea was the answer. Even on good days, he insisted that tea simply made them better. Tea, he insisted, brought people together. Couple's drank it in bed together, friends could chat and laugh and catch up after a long parting with it, long unexpected evenings in waiting rooms were lessened in their disruption by the presence of tea.

Coffee? No, coffee was for Americans, he said. Coffee was too fast, too hardcore, too rushed, too complicated. It was bitter and made his nose hairs itch, and these fancy lattes and mochas and cappuccinos were more like hot milkshakes than anything else. And a frappe? What the fuck was a frappe?

Tea was slow, calming; delicately made. Tea required patience and a deep sigh after the first sip. Tea was good with cake or biscuits, or just after a nice meal, to let your gut know that you're all finished. Tea was good.

Mickey and Marcus had shared many an evening, afternoon, morning, late night, sipping from mugs, listening to the shopping channels on the TV, and talking about nothing and everything, all at once. There was nothing they couldn't talk about – the time they spent together always passed quicker than expected. The clock showed times that were bafflingly far apart when it felt like not long had passed at all. Time was wicked, in that sense. In the most joyous moments, it would snatch back every spare second and leave you feeling like there was never enough. In the awkward, tense, awful moments, time was far too gracious and giving with the length of the minutes that passed. Extracting a tooth, breaking up with someone, being told his father was dead – those were the longest moments of Marcus's life, to date.

"I wonder who *did* do it then," Marcus said, as the two sat and pondered.

"I dunno, kid. The coppers wouldn't tell me naffin'. Just asked questions, wrote down whatever I said in a little notebook. Din't bovver me – they've not come knockin' again, so that's all I'm glad for."

"I heard he had a wife and kids." Marcus said, sadly.

"Yeah?"

"Yeah, three little ones. Awful, isn't it? How strange as well. Some random guy in sunny suburbia gets shot down in his own garden. I think I'd heard his name before. he sounds a decent enough bloke really. Maybe he was just in a bad mood when you spoke to him?"

"Maybe, yeah. People can 'ave their rough days, I s'pose."

"Normally it's in like the dodgy end of town that you hear about these murders and fights and bad things happening – people that, like, deserve it, y'know? The ones that are involved in drugs and prostitutes and stuff like that. People who are asking for it?" Marcus shook his head, "But he works for a bank and he's nice to his neighbours. What's anybody got out of knocking him off?"

Mouse curled his lip into a frown. He, too, shook his head and sipped his tea.

"I hope they find him," Marcus went on.

"Hmm?"

"Whoever did it."

"Yeah, yeah, I'm sure they will, son."

"It's just not right, is it? That young wife of his has got to raise those kids all by herself now. How awful. What if the kids saw it as well – him, I mean. When he was found and that? What if they looked out the bedroom window or something? That would have just been horrific."

Mickey sighed a deep sigh and frowned, "You're right, it would be awful. But we don't know the full story, do we. They'll be a reason he was found dead, and they'll be a reason someone pulled that trigger. Him that done it will no doubt have had his reasons – kiddies or not. I don't think I've ever heard of a man killin' someone without good reason. It's just too much of a risk, too much to lose, unless you got good reason for it. You never know – maybe the world is a better place without Robert Brooker in it?"

Marcus nodded, "Yeah, maybe."

They cascaded back into a heavy silence. Mouse sipped his tea and stared ahead, at his living room wall. He didn't say another word.

CHAPTER 16

Mouse waited for Marcus to leave. He didn't stay for long – he had work and wanted to see if he could catch Jane at lunch time, too, so wouldn't be returning, he assured. But the two spent a good hour or so watching the TV and discussing the news headlines and drinking tea.

"I might come 'round tomorrow though, if you're free?" Marc said, as he stood up from the soft embrace of the sofa cushions. He pulled his jeans down, as they had all bunched up around his thighs from where he'd been sat for so long. He re-adjusted the collar of his leather jacket, after popping his empty mug in the sink in the kitchenette. There was no other washing up to be seen whatsoever within the entire flat.

"Yeah, I'm at work in the mornin' – matinee showing – but should be home by 'bout four?"

"Awesome."

He left. Mouse closed the door behind him and watched through the peep hole to ensure he had disappeared all the way down the corridor. He saw Marcus turn towards the stairs and listened to hear the pattern of his footsteps as he pattered down them. He waited to see if he could hear him reach the next set of stairs. He listened further, to make sure he wasn't coming back up. He listened a little while longer – pressing his ear against the surface of the wood, holding his breath and turning his focus inward, in order to tune out all his other senses.

Okay, he was gone.

Mouse carefully turned the key in the lock, put the chain across, and turned off the latch. If he had a dead bolt, he would have used that, too. He paused once more, his entire body rigid, not even blinking, as he once again checked he was alone.

The living room was neat, tidy, and flawless. Everything had its place. Mickey had done this out of anxiousness and a little bit of boredom. He had needed something to keep his hands busy whilst he organised his thoughts the previous evening. He wasn't sure whether or not he wanted to maintain this level of organisation. Was it wiser to keep things tidy? Or would it make more sense to create a bigger mess? He debated it for a very long moment as he stared at the space.

No. He would leave it as it was...for now.

He walked over to the window and looked out at the landscape. His building was opposite just another apartment block. The tones of dull orange brick and black mould markings caused by excessive moisture were all he could see, really. It did not allow a lot of light to access the room. It gave the whole apartment a dull filter of grey, almost, as it was constantly in shadow. A lone pigeon sat on the window ledge, cooing softly, and consistently. Mouse found the bird irritating and shooed it away.

He looked at the window opposite. The cracking white paint around the frame, the antisocial blinds that were pulled up only half-way, and not in a way that was straight, either. He caught a glimpse of the life of the person who lived there: a family of three, by the looks of it. Mouse had seen them several times before, just in passing, but had never witnessed them in the outside world before – only ever through two panes of glass. They were a pleasant family, reasonably quiet, kept themselves to themselves. All he knew was that they celebrated Christmas, and that the father within the home had a job that required him to wear a suit. Mouse presumed, from her apron, that the mother was a waitress. The child was a girl, often dressed in pink. She had chocolate-brown skin and jet-black braided hair, just like her parents. Mouse had never looked at them often enough to know how old she was. Today, the window had a little vase on it, with a handful of yellow roses. They were wilted, somewhat. Mouse guessed that, in fact, they had been there for a fair few days – he had just neglected to notice.

He tightened the muscles round his eyes slightly and pulled the curtains too.

Mouse walked again towards the front door – checked the peep hole. Checked for noise.

Nothing.

He nodded to himself: good.

He then walked back into the living room, and headed towards the sofa, where Marcus had been sitting. He took off the throw cushions, followed by the seat cushions, and placed them neatly on the floor, to one side.

He went to the kitchenette and opened his cutlery drawer.

No.

The utensil drawer?

Yes.

He took out both a serrated knife and a carving knife, unsure of what blade exactly he would need. He took them to the sofa, and slowly lowered his old knees onto the ground. They felt like they squeaked slightly as he lowered himself down, and protested at being against a hard, cool surface such as the floor. He shushed his inner complaints and continued to work.

First, he took the carving knife, and, carefully, pushing down the fabric, so he could reach beneath the back of the sofa, he made an incision. Mindful of the springs and the sofa frame, he worked around them. Then, he pushed the cotton stuffing around within.

Would it work?

He smiled to himself. He was confident that it would.

CHAPTER 17

The first time Felix had broken the law, he was just seven years old.

"Go on, Fred: *do it.*"

He had been wearing his school uniform. He had rolled up the white sleeves of his shirt to around his elbows and taken off his tie and blazer. He had shoved them into his rucksack, which was discarded on the grass, not far away. His mum would be so angry that he hadn't rolled or folded it – she spent half an hour each weak ironing out the creases that he insisted on making. He had grey shorts on, which showed off his pale, skinny knees – one of which was badly scuffed from falling over on the tarmac the week before. The scab was itchy, but he ignored it.

Felix had hesitated, "But I could get into trouble."

"Ha-ha! Fred's a *wuss.*" One of the other boys jeered. There were five or six of them, he couldn't quite remember. They had all crowded around to watch. The added pressure made him feel nauseous and exposed.

"Yeah, Fred's a *girl.*"

"I am not!"

"*Do it* then," the first boy hissed, "*prove* you're not a girl."

Fred gulped and looked at what he could see before him. They were at the local park, not far from the playground with the swing set and the see-saw. A boy and his sister had arrived to play together. The boy was of a similar age to the group. The girl being quite a few years younger. The boy was very good though: he had perhaps promised their mother or father that he would make sure the two of them were safe at the park, and that they had fun together. She asked him if he would push her on the swings first. He was very polite and said yes, of course, but he wanted to choose what they went to play on next.

The boy and his sister had arrived on bikes. His was bright red, with flames painted all the way down the crossbar. There were black and red beads on the spokes of the wheels, which span and clicked as the wheel turned around and around. On the black bicycle seat, was the print of an eagle, with a bright yellow pointed beak, and large brown outstretched wings that hugged either side of it. Its face was angry and cunning.

Felix and his friends had all noticed the bike when the two children had arrived to play. They had all commented on how it was so *cool* – especially with the painting of the flames and the eagle. And what a lovely shade of red it was, too. Oh, yes. All of them were quite taken by it indeed.

"But I don't *need* a bike," Felix had said. It was the truth, but it came out disguised as a feeble excuse. He walked everywhere, and everywhere was really not that far away.

"So? But you want it. You said you wanted it, Fred."

"I do."

"Then go and *take it.*"

There was a little bit of a scuffle. Felix was shoved from behind, unexpectedly, and he wobbled slightly, managing to catch his footing before he stumbled. He turned back to look at the other boys, who all nodded in anticipation and eagerness. They waved for him to continue forward.

"Higher, Jon, *higher!*" The girl was saying as she sat on the swing. The two of them had their back to Felix as he walked closer.

"I'm *trying!*" Jon laughed, and shoved the swing even harder, so that the chains flipped back slightly as he pushed her.

Felix stood next to the bikes, creeping along to try and remain unheard. He was right next to them now. He looked down at the shiny red paint and the eagle's cunning smile. It really was a beautiful bike and looked pretty much brand-new. It was the height of summer, so he guessed it wasn't a gift from Father Christmas. More likely a recent birthday present…

Fred looked back at his friends. His cheeks felt flushed from embarrassment and uncertainty. They still held a childish chubbiness in them.

"C'mon!" One of the boys yelled, "Just take it already!"

Jon and his younger sister both looked round, and Felix was faced with a very sudden snap decision. He was ashamed of the choice he made, but went through with it anyway, as he grabbed the handles of the bike, and, whilst running, swung his legs over it and began to peddle.

The group of boys all burst into hysterics at seeing their friend's face filled with so much fear. Felix didn't even look behind him as he raced down the path, through the park. He just wanted to get away from the situation, as best he could.

Little did he know that Jon had taken it upon himself to borrow his younger sister's bike and chase after him – causing the group of boys to hurl themselves on the floor with laughter, at the sight of a seven-year-old using a five-year-old's bike. Racing down the park pathway on a bright pink and sparkly bicycle, complete with a wicker basket on the front and tassels on the handlebars.

Fred peddled and peddled and felt grateful that his friends had let him borrow their bikes before in order to learn how to cycle at all. He imagined what could have happened if he couldn't have gotten away so fast – that would have been disastrous. He imagined that the boy would have probably wanted to fight him and might have punched him in the face. Felix didn't like the idea of that. He kept going.

He cycled down the hill and came towards the bit of the path that was closest to the river below. There was a bridge approaching, a bridge with only a very shallow wall between the path and the rushing waters below, and Felix reached for the brakes.

And then he saw him – the boy, Jon – approaching from the opposite end of the bridge. He'd clearly gone around the other way in order to stop him and block his path.

"Hey!" Jon shouted, "That's my bike!"

Felix juddered to a holt and the two boys stopped only inches away from each other.

"Give it back." Jon said.

"No."

"But it's *mine*."

"I found it. It's my bike. Besides, you've already got one."

"This is my sister's. I had to chase you to get you to stop."

Felix still felt the sting of his friends' words. He heard them in his head, calling him nasty names and mocking him, "No. You're just a *girl*. You shouldn't have a red bike if you're a girl."

The boy went red in the face and huffed, angrily. "Fine." He said, "But my dad is a policeman. And I'm going to tell him what you did, and you stole it, so that's theft so you'll go to *jail*."

Felix didn't know much about jail. He didn't know much about the police, either. He also didn't know that police officers didn't make a habit of sending children to jail for things such as this. So, when Felix was threatened with going to jail and of the police being told, Felix got very, very scared.

"I won't let you tell him." Felix said, getting off the bike. He dumped it on the floor and rolled his sleeves up some more. Felix stood in front of Jon and his face was very angry. Jon's face was angry, too.

"Even if you give it back, I'm going to tell him, because you still stole it and that's against the law."

Fred felt within him a rage build that he had only ever felt in a few instances before. It was an overwhelming feeling of very strong emotions, emotions he was still too young and small to be able to contain. He had felt it when he had been shoved over in the playground and was embarrassed and angry. He had felt it when he had been grounded for getting grass-stains on his school trousers for a fourth time. He had felt it when his favourite toy was broken and could not be fixed.

The river below roared hungrily, Felix could hardly hear his own thoughts over the noise of it as it gushed by. Twigs and leaves and other missing parts of nature all got washed away downstream.

Felix let out an uncontainable yell, roaring along with the waters, and reached out and shoved Jon, as hard as he could. He used all his mite, all his emotions, and he closed his eyes and just shoved him, with everything he'd got.

Jon, already with his feet very close to the shallow wall, stumbled backwards. The back of his knees hit the top of the wall, and he continued to fall. Back, back, back he went. Felix watched, and it was as if the whole scene, which lasted no more than three seconds, was in slow motion.

He saw Jon's face go from angry, to fear, to realisation, to… gone.

Felix blinked.

He was alone on the bridge. The water in the river frothed and bubbled and rushed away. There was no trace of Jon.

Felix felt himself begin to take deep breaths that he wasn't in control of – deep breaths that came and went in quick succession. He felt his heart racing in his ribcage from the adrenaline of it all. His forehead was slick with sweat and he pushed his dark hair backwards, out of the way, so it lay flat against the rest of his head. His legs felt weak and wobbly and he wanted to sit down.

Felix looked around him at the trees and at the water and at the two bikes that now lay abandoned on the path.

Without really thinking all that much, he picked them up. One by one, he threw them into the river. He didn't want the red bike anymore. Felix didn't want to look at either of the bikes. He didn't want anybody to find them.

He thought he could hear the beating footsteps of his five friends as they ran to catch up with him. Their laughter echoed through the trees. Felix could hear their conversations about how funny the whole thing had been, and how they wanted to see Felix and the other boy in a fight over the red bike. But before they could catch a glimpse of him, Felix made sure he was out of sight. He ran, and he ran, and he ran, and he didn't stop running until it was dark, and the weather was getting cold. He did not go home. He did not go to his friends' houses. He didn't know where to go at all. All he knew was that he had to run away, and run far, and start a new life, somewhere else. Nobody would believe him or listen to him. It was an accident, but grown-ups never believed that, when he'd told them so before. And this was very serious. There was only one person he knew he could talk to, and that was his brother. But his brother would be at home, with their mother. And he knew that if mother found out what he had done, he was sure to be grounded for a hundred years.

That evening, the little girl had been taken home by the police, in tears. Jon's family had been told that their son had been reported missing, and that both of the bikes were missing, too. They had asked the little girl what she saw, and she recounted, in between sobs, the story of the boys chasing one another on the bikes. The police had promised they would continue the search. The same thing happened at Felix's house. His mum went from being annoyed at him for being so late for dinner, to muffling her sobs into a tea towel on the dining room floor.

A few days later, at a calmer point in the river, the two bikes were discovered. Both Felix's and Jon's families were told.

And it was a few days after that when, what was believed to be Jon, was uncovered from the banks of the river, some miles down. His body was ashen white and swollen from where the water had been around him for almost a week. He'd sucked it up like a sponge. There was very little way of identifying him, except for the clothes he wore. His parents were brought in to identify the body and confirmed what the detectives thought to be true.

It was later that day that the police, once more, went to see Felix's family. They sat his mum down and told her what had been uncovered and that, although Fred had still not been found, they presumed the same fate had met her son, too.

Felix's brother was confused and said he didn't believe Fred would have been washed away. He didn't believe Fred was silly enough to ride a bike into a river.

His mother had patted his head, combed his hair with her fingers, clutched him tightly to her. She had explained that she didn't think so either, but that it was the truth and that his brother was gone.

Felix's brother didn't cry, but instead pondered.

"I don't believe it," He said, decisively.

"I know, Mouse," she answered, as she cried and cradled him in her arms as the two stood in the living room, "me neither."

CHAPTER 18

Mouse remembered when he had been seven years old, laying in his bed, and looking across the room to the empty bed that now existed next to him.

The first night without Fred there was the strangest. He remembered the night when he didn't come home. He remembered the sausage and mash that had been plated up for him had just sat on the dining table all evening, going cold. Their mother had thrust it down on the table, to begin with:

"If he's not back home to eat his dinner when it's ready, then he'll eat it *cold.*" She spat. Mickey had tucked into his without so much as batting an eyelid. He wanted warm food – and knew how quickly mash potato appeared to lose its heat, especially if not covered with lashings of scalding-hot gravy. He'd made sure he was home on time and knew that his mother was often just a bit angry and didn't mean the things she said. He was very right on this occasion as well, because as soon as the street-lamps came on outside, and it began to get dark, and the police were knocking on the door, his mother was in a right state. She couldn't compose herself long enough to make the officer's a cup of tea. Mickey had done that for them. He had been told he was very good at making tea.

His mother was just very in-touch with her emotions, that was all.

Mickey remained very calm when the police had arrived.

And, despite being shunned from the room to begin with (as his mum haphazardly waved a tea towel in the direction of the door) he had stayed outside in the hallway, and pressed his ear against the door, and listened to what was being said. Again, he wasn't in a great deal of shock. It was more confusion, as something about what they were saying just didn't seem to add up. Of course, he knew he could be wrong, and Mickey had often been wrong. But at the same time this was his brother they were on about, and the two of them were closer than anything. If anybody knew Fred, it was Mickey. And Mickey just couldn't really believe that Fred would be stupid enough, in any circumstance, to fall – no, not fall, *ride a bike* - into a river and drown as a result. Fred was a feisty bugger at the best of times. If he was riding a bike, it wouldn't be in a way that would make him fall into the river – *especially* in a way for another idiot kid to fall into the river behind him. Or, even more unlikely, he would *definitely* not have followed said idiot kid into a river, if the other had gone in first.

He looked over at the empty bed again. This was a week later now, when the bikes and the other boy had been discovered. Again, Mickey stood by his word. He did not get upset like his mother did. He did not cry. He did not agree to make funeral arrangements with an empty coffin, in memory of his brother. Because, Mickey was sure, his brother was not dead.

There was a tapping noise.

Was it the window?

Mickey sat up in his bed. The room was very dark, very narrow – they lived in a terrace house you see. The two single beds were less than two feet away from one another, really. Mickey swung his legs over the edge of the bed – and listened.

Lots of silence...Lots of darkness...

Tap-tap-tap

The noise was gentle. Quiet.

Quiet on *purpose*.

Mickey shot out of bed and ran to the window. He pulled back the curtains and, low and behold, true to his instincts, there, on the windowsill, sat Fred.

He grinned at him from the opposite side of the glass and pressed a finger to his lips – *sshh*. He then pointed to the windowpane and urged Mickey to open it. Without any hesitation, Mickey undid the latch, and pulled up the glass.

He didn't even say a word as he pulled his brother through the window and into an embrace. He squeezed him tightly, and felt all of his ribs, even through his clothing. He looked pale and tired, but equally pleased to see him.

"Where have you *been?!*" Mickey asked him. He was excited, he was fidgety. It was like on Christmas mornings when they would wake up way before the allotted Christmas-morning-start-time of seven-thirty. There had been many a Christmas when the two boys would set an alarm for three in the morning instead, and sneak downstairs to see if the presents were out and ready yet. They would sit every year on one bed and open their stocking-fillers together.

Fred, despite his dishevelled appearance, had a huge smile on his face.

"I've been in hiding!" He answered, "It's the longest game of hide and seek I've ever played!"

"But why are you hiding?" Mickey asked.

"It's a very long story, really," Fred scratched his head. He hopped onto his bed and jiggled up and down on the springy mattress, "Ooh, this is so *soft*. I forgot how soft it was." He smoothed his hand over the layers of blankets and lay his head down on the pillow and let out a laugh, "Haha!" he was deliriously giddy on the most basic of home comforts.

"I've missed you," Mickey said, "I knew you weren't dead – I *knew* it!"

"Haha, no, of course I'm not dead. I've missed you too, Mouse. It's been very tricky really. I didn't want to run away. But I had to."

"But why?"

It was a loaded question – more loaded than Mickey realised, at that moment. In retrospect, when he looked back as an older man, he realised that if Felix had never returned that night, if he had never stopped by to say hi and explain himself, then Mickey's life might have taken a different turn. He probably would have continued to love his life, along with his mother. He would have eventually agreed with the masses and presumed that his brother had drowned in the river when he was just a boy. He probably would have stayed in school, and, as he was very smart, might have gotten better grades and gotten a better job as a manager a company, or even started his own. He never saw himself as smart enough to be a doctor or a lawyer or any of those big-big-brain jobs. But he could be a manager, for sure. Or maybe a therapist. Maybe he would be earning a *salary* and have *sick pay*, rather than working for minimum wage and scraping gum off the bottom of auditorium seats on Saturday afternoons.

"Okay, I'll tell you the truth, Mouse. But only because you're my brother. And only because I know I can trust you the most in the whole wide world. I can trust you, can't I?"

Micky nodded.

"Cross your heart and hope to die?"

Mickey nodded again and traced his finger across his chest in the shape of an X. "Hope to die." He said.

Fred then took a very deep breath, and he told him. He told him everything. He told him about the boys and how they were pushing him to do something bad. He told him about the bike and how beautiful it was. He told him about the little girl and the boy, Jon. He told him about the chase, and the argument, and the shove...

"You *pushed* him?" Mickey was shook. His eyes were wide, and his mouth gaped wide open.

"I didn't *mean* to," Fred insisted, "I didn't, I swear I didn't mean to. It was an accident. I just got...so, so *angry* and I just pushed him. I didn't even mean to do it!"

Fred's reply was, really, just the same statement, repeated several different ways, but the boy really did look afraid and sorry for what he had done. He was so scared that he would get into trouble, Mickey could see it in his eyes. And Mickey understood why. It wasn't just petty theft between schoolboys that was going on now. This was *murder*. Manslaughter. Fred had *killed* someone.

"I don't know what the law says about kids killing people," Mickey said, scratching his head, "and I don't suppose we can really ask anybody about it, either."

"NO, no – we can't ask anybody. *You* can't *tell* anybody I was even *here*. Right?"

Mickey nodded again, calmly, as he sat and thought, "I don't think they'd send you to prison though. We're not grownups or anything. And it *was* an accident."

"But the boy – Jon – he said his dad was a police officer. And he said that he was gonna send me to jail for stealing the bike, so, so, so" – Fred tripped over his words in his panic – "if he can do that then what would he be able to do for me...*killing someone.*"

"But we're just kids!"

"But the law is the law, isn't it? They don't change it just because you're seven!"

The two boys sat on their respective beds, opposite each other. The room was still dark, they hadn't turned on any of the lights, and they spoke in hushed tones so as not to wake their mother. It felt dastardly to be awake, *way* past their bedtime, talking about murder and prison and theft in the middle of the night. It was a strange feeling because, in one sense, they were just the same as they always were – two boys, talking about things they shouldn't be, in the dark, just being boys, being brothers. That's what kids do.

But manslaughter...aiding and abetting a murderer...faking your own death...

That's not what kids do.

"I can't stay." Fred said.

The two boys were sad. They both knew why. They both knew it was what had to be done.

"But...where will you go?"

"I'm not sure. Far away, probably."

"I'll come with you."

"No, Mouse. You have to stay here. Mum would have no heart left if neither of us were here."

"But..." Mickey felt so lost. He couldn't bear the thought of never seeing his brother again. He just couldn't bear it. He couldn't bear the thought of being without him, not knowing where he was, or what he was up to. He also couldn't bear the thought of being the only son for their already-overly-emotional mother. They had no father around for her to busy herself with. And their mother made jokes that not even the milkman (who wasn't especially handsome) was interested in seeing what her bedsheets looked like. She'd go into overdrive with loneliness and control and would smother Mickey to death by accident with her gigantic bosom when she hugged him ever-too-tightly.

The night Fred had been announced as presumed-dead, their mother had clung onto Mickey so tightly he thought his own ears would pop off.

"I'm never going to let you go again, Mickey, never! You are never, ever leaving my sight, or my arms, ever again!" she had said, as she sobbed into his hair.

Oh, how he wished he could have loosened her at that point, even just by a little bit.

"It hurts so much," She had whimpered, "You two... you've always been together. He's your brother, your twin...I carried you together for nine whole months...you shared every-thing – even my womb!"

Mickey did not know what a womb was but thought that now was not the best time to ask.

"You look just like him, too..." She had said this last part with a smile. A sad smile. A bitter-sweet smile.

Bing. Back to the present moment.

"Fred, wait!" Mickey stood up, eager and alert, "I have an idea!"

CHAPTER 19

"**D**o you have any siblings, Mouse?" Olwyn asked.

It was Monday, and the two of them stood together on the stairwell at the theatre. It was a long, four-storey-high staircase, grandeur, in fact. The walls were painted a vibrant shade of white – the kind of white that, if a ray of golden sun hit it, the sunlight would bounce right back and blind you, outright. Thankfully, the early morning was overcast, and so the two workers could see what they were doing most happily. The carpet beneath their feet was old and not as springy as it once had been. Several pairs of feet – stilettoes, peep-toes, sling-backs, T-straps, brogues, loafers, oxfords and monks – all gently stamping down the fibres of the carpet, steadily, over the years.

Mickey and Olwyn both had a cloth each, and a tub of brass-cleaner between them. Along the staircase, on both sides, all the way up, was a golden-gleaming bannister. The parts of the bannister where the pair had already worked were, naturally, the most gleaming of them all.

Mickey pondered the question. At first thought maybe he could just ignore it and pretend he didn't hear. But they were the only two within the building, aside from the odd member of management or two. But they were squirrelled away up in the office, out of sight. The place, despite being so large and vacant, was surprisingly not really that open to allowing echoes.

"Siblings?" Mouse repeated, "Nah. None. Only child. 'Ow 'bout you?"

CHAPTER 20

Marcus walked down the staircase of Jane's house. He had been lucky enough to now have been gifted a key. It was so when she left at five o'clock that morning for her early Hot Yoga class, Marcus was free to have another two hours in bed, and then lock up behind him. He wasn't entirely sure what Hot Yoga was. He had presumed it was done naked. But when he had said this to her, Jane had laughed so hysterically that she didn't have the breath left to explain it properly.

The air was clean and clear and especially frosty that morning. The pavement beneath his feet was littered with the glistening of tiny ice crystals. It was as if someone had run down the street sprinkling fine glitter everywhere. The grass, too, was crunchy underfoot. It was a noise that made him linger as he walked, to savour the sound.

Marcus felt glad that he and Mickey had straightened things out again. It had been a scary few days. Thinking that the man he was so close friends with was, in fact, not really the man he thought he was – it had bothered him. But having sat down with him and talked with him, he realised that it was just his paranoia and over-active imagination working overtime.

Sure, he knew Mickey was *capable* of taking the life of another. But, like he said, it just wasn't conducive. It wasn't *realistic.* Why would he? Why would he do that? There was just no point to it. Mickey didn't even know the man.

As he waited at the bus stop, Marcus noticed across the road the man who lived in the flat opposite Mouse. He wore a beautiful knee-length duster which, Marcus imagined, although nice to look at, could not be protecting the man from the cold especially well. He had parked his car on this road overnight, it seemed, and was now proceeding to scrape ice away from the windscreen with an old loyalty card that he'd found in his wallet. Marcus held a small laugh in his throat – the neighbour couldn't be *that* loyal then, really, if he was willing to sacrifice his loyalty in order to get to work on time.

The bus ride was hot and sweaty, with all the people with all their many layers of unflattering wool and waterproofs. The windows steamed up and Marcus felt a childish urge to draw in the condensation. In a way which he thought was not very noticeable, he drew a tiny smiley face. He smiled back at it.

Yes, he thought. Today was a good day.

"Fucking ridiculous this is, isn't it?" The old lady he sat next to piped up.

Marcus turned around, confused, "I'm sorry?"

"This!" She batted the newspaper she was reading with the opposite hand, "They still don't know who's bloody done it. They've got no clue!"

Marcus looked down at the newspaper and read the title: STILL NO LEADS ON BROOKER MURDERER, POLICE CONFIRM

"It's only been a week or so," Marcus said, "These things take time. They have nothing to go off. Nobody saw anything."

"I don't believe that for one minute!" Said the grumpy old lady. Her pink-lined lips twisted as if she tasted something sour. All her wrinkles squeezed together like the asshole of a cat, "*Somebody* will know *something.*" She went on, "And that somebody will have friends and family and colleagues and all sorts. It's up to *those* people to come forward if they have the information. It's awful that they don't! How hateful, hiding somebody simply because you know them, even if you know the *awful* things they've done!"

Her voice was shrill, and Marcus winced slightly. Her tone

got louder the more riled up she got.

"Just think of the family!" the old lady continued. She re-arranged a red polka-dot plastic rain-cap that she'd tied around her clearly-dyed brown curls, "Now that poor wife of his has to raise three rug rats – on her own! *Somebody* is responsible. It's awful that anybody should be left in such a situation as she is. And why him? Why would anybody kill such a lovely family man? He wasn't harming anybody! This is cold-blooded mur-der!"

Marcus decided to phase the lady out, and just stared straight ahead as he sat on the bus. Her shrill tones continued as she went on about how unfair it was, and how the murderer was most likely a psychopath, most likely just did it for the fun of it. Marcus, at this point, really didn't care enough to hold up the feeble conversation, and he made no attempt to do so.

It was a relief, really, when the bus approached Marcus's stop and he pretended to be sorry as he squeezed past the old lady and said his goodbyes to her. She got over his absence very quickly and was soon bothering the next person who volun-teered to sit down next to her. Marcus was certain that they would equally regret their decision. He hoped the smiley face he had left on the window would bring them some sort of joy, or distraction.

The walk from the bus stop to the garage was only a short one. He could pretty much see it as soon as he stepped down off the bus and said thank you to the driver. What he was most pleased by was that it appeared Mickey was already at the gar-age that morning – maybe he'd come to say good morning to him, on his own way to work. Did they normally have matinee shows on at the theatre on a Monday?

Mickey had his back to him as he approached, and Marcus thought about taking the opportunity to scare him. He kept his footsteps as light as possible on the frosty pavement as he walked. As he got closer, he could hear the conversation that Mickey was having with the other workers at the garage.

"I don't know what's up with it," Mickey was saying,

"Keeps cutting out on me every now and again, but it's not the fuel – it's a petrol motor, but I never put diesel in it or anything. Just every so often it'll lose power. Don't know if it's possibly something to do with the cambelt?"

Marcus found this odd – Mickey knew a great deal about motors, but he did not have a car himself.

"No worries, sir, just leave it with us," Darrel. It was Marcus's colleague Darrel that he was speaking to. Marcus recognised his voice, "Give us a day or so to look at it and we'll give you a call to let you know what we find out."

"Great stuff," He shook Darrel's hand.

"Just need a name and phone number, sir?"

He reeled off the number. Marcus was surprised when it was not a phone number he recognised – Mickey had had the same house phone since the day they'd met, and his contact number had never once changed.

"That's great," Darrel went on. He had a very good customer-service voice, chirpy and aloof and full of enthusiasm that could only be likened to someone on an infomercial, "And what name shall I put it under, sir?"

"Felix."

There was a pause as Darrel scribbled down the name, "That's all booked in for you, sir. We'll let you know how she gets on."

"Ta very much."

Marcus stood, very confused, as the man swivelled around on the spot to face him. It was Mickey. It was definitely Mickey. The eyes that stared back at him, the moustache, the smirk – it was all exactly the same.

"Alrigh', son?" He said, and gave him a pat on the shoulder, very gently, very friendly, and then carried on with his business. He was halfway down the street before Marcus could break the trance he was in.

"Darrel?"

"Alright, Marc? How's things with that girl of yours–?"

"Who was that man?"

"Some guy called Felix, got a broken Beamer –"

"And it's *his* car?"

"I believe so. He said it was his, yeah."

"I need to sit down."

Marcus slumped onto the pavement in amazement, and then turned back to look at the mysterious man.

But, just as magically as he had appeared in Marc's life, the mysterious doppelgänger of Mickeys, was gone.

CHAPTER 21

The two boys had made their plan.

Mickey had thought it up and explained every-thing. Fred had sat in amazement, equally excited at the thought of it all. It was perfect. It was the perfect way for the two of them to continue to live the same life – but a sure-fire way for Fred to know he would never be sent to jail for the murder of another boy.

It was crazy to think neither of them had thought of it sooner. There were so many instances when they were even younger when they could have made the most of looking identical to one another. They could have swapped clothes, tricked people, played all sorts of games and pranks on their friends, their mother – and especially the teachers at school. It now all made sense why they had purposefully been put into separate classes.

"We need to pack a rucksack for you," Mickey said, "With lots of things to help us when we're out and about – and a spare set of clothes of mine so you can look like me whenever you need to."

Fred nodded and they both started searching the room for things of Mickey's that they could afford to share. In went a big, thick blanket, a duffle coat, a set of shorts and a long pair of jeans. Then, one full set of his school uniform, a baseball hat ("Because everyone in disguise in the movies always wears a baseball cap and sunglasses"). They both decided that pyjamas were a bit useless, so they stayed out. Fred couldn't choose which t-shirt he liked best, so he took three. He also took his toothbrush, because their mother was always insistent that the boys *must* clean their teeth twice a day, else they will all fall out.

"What will you tell her if she notices all these things are missing?"

Mickey thought for a second. His brain was doing an awful lot of thinking this evening.

"I think I'll tell her I threw it away. Or that I gave it away to a charity, because I was too sad looking at it all the time… yeah; that sounds like something she would say, so she must believe it."

Fred nodded, "Cool. I like it."

And it was on that evening, the first of many, that Fred disappeared out of the window, into the night, to find a place to stay, knowing that he would very soon be returning home.

They kept up this façade for several, several years.

It was incredible how often they should have gotten caught but didn't. It showed something of their talents. They were quite good, for the most part, at switching identities. But it was also down to the sheer dumbness of the society that surrounded them as to why things weren't questioned more. Mickey would ask to go to the toilet then return less than a minute later – nobody asked why his urination schedule was so short, or so frequent. Nobody realise that Mickey would enter the bathroom just as Fred was exiting it, wearing the same clothing. It was especially easy when it came to school, what with them both having matching sets of the required uniform. The two young boys loved it. They didn't have to stay in a class for very long if they were bored. They didn't have to go to school for five days a week, either. They split it in half, did fifty-fifty. It was brilliant for them – however, not so brilliant for their growing minds, and their grades.

Their mother sat one of them down one evening to have a

word:

"Mickey, I'm awfully worried," She said, "Some weeks you have excellent marks on your tests, and some weeks you're inches away from being kicked out of school! Is everything okay? Are you struggling?"

Mickey – or was it Fred? – nodded, "I just miss Fred so much. I keep thinking about him. It makes me distracted."

And after that short conversation their mother had pulled him in close, sobbed and sobbed and sobbed onto his shoulder, and said she fully understood. There was no pressure to do well in school. The following morning, she rang up and spoke to the Head Mistress, explained the matter, and Mickey/Fred was suddenly exempt from taking formal academic examinations.

The boys couldn't believe their *luck*.

It was from here that it began to excel, however. With less time required for learning, Fred began to ask Mickey about their future, and how exactly they should continue to live the way they did, forever.

"How will it work when we're old?" He asked, "What if you want to do one job, but I don't like it? Grown-ups need money to pay for things, don't they?"

"It will be okay," Mickey said, "We don't have to worry about that yet – let's just keep going as we are, and we can worry about being grown-ups when we *are* grown-ups."

Fred shook his head, "No, Mickey. I've been thinking. And I've come up with an idea."

The two of them were sat on the very top-top of a hill, next to a busy road. Behind them there was a dense woodland, where they had walked through in order to get to where they were now. They couldn't hang out together at the park anymore, in case somebody noticed them together. Up here, well out of the way of anybody else, the two boys were free to be together, outside, and not have anybody recognise them. If anyone looked up from the road, they would not be close enough to see that their faces matched.

"What's your idea? We're not going to run away, are we?"

"No, no...well...maybe."

Mickey looked shocked at the idea, and thoroughly confused. They were both nine now. The façade had been continuing for two years, and everybody had moved on from the idea of Fred passing. It still made their mother tremble and weep, but the rest of the town was at peace with the idea.

"Well, I was thinking, we can't really continue like this forever – I'm going to get too big to hide under the bed, like I do now. And I can't walk around this town without being recognised. I need money, and...I've already committed crimes before, when I shoved that boy on the bridge..."

"Fred, *no*. What are you even talking about? We've got a good system going here! You can't put all this effort into avoiding going to jail and then try and start a life committing *more* crimes! You're crazy!"

"Well what you don't know is that I've already been doing it!"

The sentence echoed quietly off the hillside. Mickey felt it echo in his head, as well.

"You've been doing *what?*"

"I've been stealing. I've been going into shops and stealing food for us. And I've been taking people's lunch money at school. And I've even stolen a lady's handbag on the bus, once."

Mickey couldn't believe his ears. His eyes went wide and he pressed his hands to either side of his face in despair, "Fred, *why?* Why would you do that? Why would you do that, *dressed as me!*"

"It's not like I did it *just* for me, or just for fun or anything!" He protested. He was getting angry too now, "Whenever I take something, I always make sure you get half of it, too. We share everything, Mouse. You're my brother, we're the best of friends in the whole wide world! There isn't anything I wouldn't do for you!"

"But, *Fred* –!"

"Are you saying you wouldn't do anything in the world for

me, too?"

"No, but –"

"If you asked *me* to do this for *you,* I wouldn't even *hesi-tate.* You're my brother, I would do *anything* for you – I would *always* say yes. So obviously I must care about you more than *you* care about *me.*"

"That's not true!"

"Then why won't you agree to this, when it will clearly work?"

Mickey sat for a moment, listening to the cars whizz by and the lorries roar past on the large road below them. The wind was getting colder and the sun was threatening to set. Slowly, he nodded, and looked down at the grass they were sat on. His bum was getting cold from sitting cross-legged on the chill ground.

"Okay," He agreed, if half-heartedly, "I'll do it. We should do it." He attempted a smile, "We'll be a crime-committing duo!"

Fred nudged him gently with his elbow, "That's the spirit!" He stood up from the ground, his shorts damp at the back from where he had been sat, and he raised his arms triumphantly into the air, "A crime-committing duo!" He shouted towards the passing traffic.

Nobody heard him, nobody looked up, of course, except from Mickey. His gaze drifted awkwardly upwards to his twin brother, to where he stood. He was less than confident about this plan of his, and about his insistence that it would work. Mickey was filled with doubt.

Nonetheless, they continued to celebrate together, before journeying the short walk home. Fred spoke of the future, filled with joy and hope. Whereas Mickey spoke of the past – his heart twinging with longing, nostalgia, and a hint of regret.

CHAPTER 22

"**M**ichael Donaldson, I am arresting you on suspicion of the murder of Robert Brooker. You do not have to say anything, but it may harm your defence if you do not mention, when questioned, something which you later rely on in court. Anything you do say may be given in evidence."

Mickey stood in his living room, the two police officers, dressed in their black and white uniforms, going through their usual routine that they follow when making an arrest. He looked at his tidy flat, his fresh cup of tea, steaming away on a coaster atop the coffee table. He had always hated how it was called a coffee table, considering he never put coffee on it. He also hated how he knew that cup of tea would still be there when – or, rather *if* – he returned. It would be stone-cold, and the milk would be congealed by then. What a waste.

They led him out of the flat and into the elevator. Mickey didn't speak, the entire time. He came quietly, quite literally. His only request was that they escorted him out of the back exit of the building, rather than the front. He understood that the handcuffs were mandatory, given what he was being arrested under suspicion of. And he knew they would not allow him to cover the handcuffs with a coat or scarf, or something similar. Originally, he could tell, they wanted to say no to his request. But given his age, given his quiet stature and his compliance, the younger officers must have taken pity on him. They agreed.

They walked him out, each with a hand on his respective elbows, and seated him in the back of the police car. The air was especially chill outside – the insistent winter not giving in for even a moment. He was grateful he had been wearing his black fleece jacket when the police officers had called at his place of residence. Its added layer, although not especially thick, kept in a much-needed warmth for his frail and aging bones.

Being in the back of a police car, driving through the busy streets on the way to the police station, reminded Mickey of a time some years ago. *Several* years ago, in fact. The sky, the streets and the air itself held a grey film over it, tainted by the circumstances, tainted by the memory.

They had been teenagers. It had been over ten years since the first time Fred and Mickey had swapped their identities. They had just left school. Mickey was looking at applying for colleges, and other types of further education – or perhaps an apprentice-ship. Fred – or *Felix* as he now insisted on being called – had other ideas.

Felix had become increasingly set in his ways as the two boys had grown up into men. Their looks were still incredibly similar, but Felix had gotten tired by being chained to Mickey's life and his reputation. He wanted to do different things, hang around with a different people…he had no interest in an edu-cation or in living a good and noble life. And he had other plans, too. He was leaning towards not going down that dark and twisted path alone, and of dragging his brother, kicking and screaming, as unwilling as he was – with him.

"Mouse. Over here."

Felix had insisted on the two of them meeting that even-ing in a back alley. It was dark and the evening was hot and humid – the stickiest summer they had ever experienced. It wasn't far from their home. Although, perhaps calling it 'home' no longer really applied to the both of them. Felix had not re-turned there in some months. He had not been to see their mother and taken the role of 'Mickey' in some time.

Mickey dug his hands deep into his pockets and dipped his head low, so he appeared stooped. He did not want to be there that evening. He had applications for college to fill out. He had promised their mother he would get up early the following morning to mow the grass for her. He had no interest in the shady business that his brother was up to.

"Alrigh'?"

Mickey nodded, "You?"

Felix nodded back, eager. His eyes had deep, dark bags beneath them, and the whites of them gleamed brightly, scarily, in the moonlight. His skin was pale, with a waxy finish to it. He was scrawnier than Mickey last remembered.

"You don't seem alright. When was the last time you ate?"

Felix shrugged, "Not important."

"I'm pretty sure it is."

"Look, listen" – Felix had a wild and erratic aura surrounding him – "I can't stay long, I have to meet someone. I've got a job. Did you bring the clothes and things that I asked for?"

Mickey regretfully took the satchel off his shoulder and slung it in Felix's direction. He scrambled for it and tore it open, searching through the contents. He looked like a hungry, unruly child with a giant bag of sweets – eagerly emptying pockets and grabbing at items with fists.

"Where's the watch?"

"What watch?"

Felix's eyes darkened and he looked equally erratic but impeccably sinister, "The list – the list that I gave you – I wrote watch on it. I need the watch that was grandpa Pete's."

"You gave me a list," Mickey agreed, "But there was no mention of a watch on it, Fred."

"Gah!" He threw his hands in the air in frustration, dropping the bag onto the floor. The clean shirts and underpants that Mickey had neatly folded were now littered in a crumpled heap on the flagstones of the alley, "Well – regardless – I need it. Get it for me."

Mickey crouched down and began to refill the satchel with the items. He didn't look at his brother when he spoke. The words that he said, he spoke them quietly, and calmly; "I'm not going to get it for you. You'll only sell it." He handed the bag to his brother once more, "Be careful, Fred. Remember: if ever you need anything, you know where to find me. Just stay out of trouble, okay?"

Mickey turned and began to walk away. The night was warm, and he was tired; his heart feeling heavy and blue from seeing his brother in such a state. He was not well. He was not himself.

"Mouse, wait," Felix said. His voice was different. He sounded calm and collected and thoughtful. His eyes, when Mickey turned to look at them, were pleading and sorrowful. It reminded Mickey of when they were children. He longed for that time to come back, knowing that it never would, "There is something you can do for me...that is, if you don't mind?"

"Anything." Mickey answered.

It was only a single word. But Mickey soon came to regret it.

"Just wait here for a second," Felix said, "I'll be back in a minute. Then we can go home, yeah? I just wanna see mum."

Mickey had been taken aback by his brother's request. But the change in heart and in personality that he saw was, admittedly, something he had been searching for now for some months. He was happy to notice even a glimmer of change, a glimmer of the same person Fred used to be.

Felix had left Mickey standing on a street corner, underneath a streetlamp. The night must have now been coming towards 4 o'clock in the morning, as just peeking over the edge of the horizon were the first tiny beams of the following day's sunlight. It had rose and orange tones to it – warm and peachy like a freshly baked fruit pie. Mickey felt a tug in his gut which he took to be a sign of hope. Although, in retrospect, it was possibly his gut trying to warn him of what was to come.

Felix disappeared around the corner, taking with him the satchel that his brother had gifted to him. He hurried down a different alleyway, where he would be entirely out of sight. He had searched through the bag one last time – still no money, nothing he could sell. His debt was higher than his eyeballs, and he knew he wouldn't be able to pay it.

He wedged the toe of his trainer into the wall and pulled himself up and over it. From here, he would be out of the way, out of visibility of anybody that would be walking past. But from where he perched, he could just about see the streetlamp under which his brother was standing.

He felt fidgety, nervous. But there was no doubt in his mind that he was going to let it happen.

Mickey saw a group of men emerge from the shadows across the street. He quickly counted them – three. That was not a number that hangs about in the early hours of the morning if they were to be doing godly business. Mickey shuffled slightly in his shoes but decided to keep his ground.

They crossed the road. They were heading directly towards him.

"Well looky here," One of them said, "I didn't think you was gonna show up."

"You what, mate?"

Mickey's confusion was ignored: "You got the money you owe me or what?"

"I don't know what the fack you're on about, mate – sorry."

Mickey dug his hands deep into his pockets and stood up tall. The gaggle of men had now approached him and were stood on the same corner as he was. They did not hesitate to get as close to him as they wanted to. Before Mickey could blink, the ring leader was stood with his face less than an inch away from his own.

"I ain't playin any fackin' games, mate" The man said. He was bald. He had an ugly scar that ran the length of his head, just above his ear.

"I ain't either. *Mate*." Mickey narrowed his eyes. He made sure not to wince. In the back of his head he was more than aware that if a fight was to break out – which it more than likely was – that he was sure to lose. But none of the Donningtons were ever raised to give up without a fight, "You're probably looking for my brother, Felix."

"HA!" The bald man had ugly teeth, too. Every single one was a bitter shade of yellow, "You think I'm gonna fall for that? You know you owe me money. It's the same thing every week with you, always trying to avoid what you know you're supposed to pay. Last week your excuse was you had a doctor's appointment. And now all of a sudden you got a twin brother, is that it?" He laughed, a wheezy, belly-laugh, "Bull*shit*. I'm having none of it"

He spat onto the pavement. Mickey took a deep and calming breath. Any second now. Here it comes...

The bald bloke lunged for him, and Mickey had, rightfully, seen it coming. He swerved to one side and watched as the hefty bloke tumbled to the floor. The other two henchmen of his didn't hesitate for a command from their leader before closing in. Mickey grabbed the wrist of the first one who attempted to punch him and bent it backwards, holding him still before plunging the base of his palm into his nose. The man recoiled in pain, and blood spurted all down his shirt.

"You think that's gonna keep me off you? Some shitty karate moves you've seen on TV? You may have killed someone, Felix, but you're not the toughest bloke on the block, are you? You're just a *kid*."

"I haven't killed anyone. And neither has Felix – that kid drowning was an accident."

"Ha! You're still trying to keep it up, ey?" The bloke was on his feet again now. He shoved the other two men aside to speak to Mickey to his face again. He wagged a threatening finger in his face, "I'm not on about the petty shit from years ago. I'm on about that girl. You know what you did. And you're kicking yourself that I watched it happen. You're working for Darius, ain't ya? He paid you to get rid of her. Now pay me my fuckin money, or I'm gonna get rid of *you*."

"I'm broke – just like your friend's nose."

The scarred man took that as an answer. The two others clenched their fists. What occurred afterwards can be summed up as a simple mess of blood and bones and sweat. Mickey, although with the knowledge of how to fight, did not know how to use his skills against three men that were, in every way, bigger than he was. He would manage to get the upper hand on one of them – tackling them to the floor then beating his elbow over and over again into their face – when another would come from behind and sweep him off his feet again. The see-saw of the fight would then topple in the opposite direction. He was passed between the three of them, each giving him a beating in turn.

Felix watched from his hiding spot, each second passing, thinking that the gang would give just one last punch, and then leave him alone.

He was wrong again, and again and again.

And that was when things got really bad.

The blue lights bounced off each of the terraced houses, illuminating the tiny backstreet neighbourhood with the echoes of the shrill and all-familiar siren. It worked like a bullet in a field full of rabbits – the men scattering like shrapnel, grabbing one another by the collar and hauling each other to their feet, scrambling down the road, their shoes beating onto the pavement with horrific speed and delusion.

Mickey lay on his back, delirious. He had red spots in his vision. His breathing was raspy, harsh.

Felix watched as the police car pulled up. Two men stepped out and were prompt in shoving Mickey so he was sitting up. They clicked handcuffs around his wrists. His scraped knuckles continued to drip blood onto the pavement behind his back.

He didn't hear all of what was said but heard the usual caution.

He was being arrested for the murder of that girl.

He didn't have to say anything

Anything he did say may be given in evidence.

They thought he was Felix.

Felix was the one who had done it.

Mickey was only half-aware of what was happening as they dragged him to his feet and shoved him on the backseat of the police car. He couldn't hear his own voice. He couldn't see for the drowning red dots that obscured his vision.

He was just nineteen years old. He protested. He thrashed. He cried out.

They took him away.

Mickey Donaldson, mistaken for the streetwise low-budget bounty hunter Felix, went to prison for seven years.

Felix's plan had worked. But it had worked too well.

CHAPTER 23

Elaine was sat on the step that led to the alley, in the back garden of their house.

She was terrified. She was beside herself with upset. This was several months before Robert Brooker was murdered. Her husband was still alive – very much so indeed. Perhaps too alive, for Elaine's liking.

She had made the mistake of getting upset with him. He had promised he would fix the toy box lid for the children, so that they didn't trap their fingers in it. The hinge needed replacing, that was all – one that stayed open when it was pushed upwards. He hadn't done it, after weeks of promising that he would. He said he would get around to it. He hadn't. And their eldest had gone to take a toy out that afternoon, and the lid had smacked down on his tiny fingers with an almighty thwack that Elaine had heard from downstairs. Elaine had been patient and loving towards the children. Kissing it better, making sure he was alright. Robert had then appeared in the doorway.

"What's all this racket?" He demanded.

"Your son just trapped his fingers in the toybox you *still* refuse to fix." Elaine snapped. She turned to their son and delicately kissed his forehead, "Are you okay, darling?" She said, gently.

Robert said nothing, but she felt his steely eyes boring into the back of her head. She kept her appearance unfaltering, gentle, kind, loving, towards the injured Christopher. He was beginning to calm down. Robert's tall and looming figure stood like he was made of stone – tall and broad shoulders. His jaw clenched, and when she looked, she noticed the muscles around the corners of his eyes and temples tighten and pulse.

"Run along now," She said to Christopher as his tears lessened. He nodded and took the teddy bear that she held out to him. He pressed it to his chest in a manner that reflected a sincere and supreme need for comfort.

Robert said nothing until the door to the playroom was gently closed behind the two of them. The hallway was dark, and Robert refused to move out of Elaine's path when she made to walk back down the stairs again.

"Why did you speak to me like that?" He said.

"Because," She heaved a sigh, "You promised to fix that broken toy box some time ago now. It's still not been done and now Cristopher has gotten hurt."

"What's with your tone?"

"My tone?"

"Your disrespectful tone. You're speaking to me like I've done something wrong."

"Darling, you do understand that our son got hurt because of your neglect to do as you said you would?"

"Neglect? You do realise I'm the person who pays for everything in this house? I'm the one who goes to work every day whilst you loiter around folding things and doing colouring-in."

Elaine pressed her lips together to hold her tongue. "I do realise that."

"Then why are you being so horrible to me?"

"I'm not being horrible," She sounded hurt and confused.

"You are. You're being nasty to me. There's no need for it."

"Darling, I would never intend to be nasty towards you, I *love* you."

He scoffed, "Yeah. Apparently."

Her mind felt confused, as if it were racing at one hundred

miles an hour. Robert had made a habit of confusing Elaine by her own words and actions. She found herself second-guessing almost all the time. She was so careful, treading on eggshells whenever she was near him, ensuring to avoid causing him any upset or need for an argument between the two of them. And then, despite her best efforts, she still found herself trying to explain her words and her actions and feeling guilty for causing a ruckus between them and their marriage.

His words stung her hard, and she withdrew from him, whilst simultaneously feeling like all she wanted to do was cocoon herself in the comfort of his strong arms and lie there until their bump-in-the-road was over.

Because he *could* be wonderful. This is what made it all the more frustrating. There were so many days, mornings, evenings, weekends, when he was so kind-hearted and so warm towards her. They had such wonderful evenings when the children were in bed when they would lie on the sofa together. She would read and he would watch television, and he would gently caress her hair absent-mindedly. Or times when they would go for walks as a family, and he would graciously reach for her hand and interlace his fingers with her own. And times when he would be so careful with her, so gentle, as if he were afraid she would break. Lifting her chin with just one finger so that he could plant a peck onto her lips or her cheek. It was moments like those where she felt the way she did when they were first together – loved and protected and at one with their marriage. This, she knew, was how she wanted it to *always* be – and why she insisted on ignoring moments like today, when he was hateful and cruel and irrational towards her.

He had said he wanted to be alone, and that it was his turn to watch the children. She had nodded, pressing her lips together again with a tight smile. She tried to stop herself from blinking because she knew it would make the tears fall. She didn't want him to accuse her of manipulating him with her "emotions" and "womanly charm". Elaine graciously left them to it and found herself aimlessly wandering around the lower rooms of the house, fidgeting with the cushions and straightening the curtains that were already straight. She opened the back door and headed out down the path. Past the green grass and the flower blossoms and the hedgerows and ended up at the back gate.

Elaine had thought about leaving, then. It was the first time she had thought of it. In all the days they had been together it was the first time she thought about simply walking away. She thought of how she could exit through the back-garden gate, walking with an air of grace and peace down the alley on the cobblestones, and simply continuing to walk and walk and walk until her feet could walk no more. Wherever her feet took her, wherever she ended up collapsing from fatigue – that was where she could begin her new life. She could leave her wedding ring and her worries, and all her belongings behind her. She could start anew. Maybe even give herself a new name... she would no longer be Mrs Elaine Brooker, and suffer the same suffering that Mrs Brooker did. She could be Ms Smith. Ms Tulip. Ms Bronte. She could be whomever she wanted to be...

Her hands, amongst her thoughts, had lifted the latch and drawn across the deadbolt on the gate, and she found herself stood on the back step that led to the alley, when her train of thought finally dumped her out at the end of its journey.

She looked at the grey cobblestones and peeped around to look at the long alleyway. She could see the end of it – one end led to the town, the other led to a long-grass field that held nothing, not even cattle, no crops. Two routes to two different destinies that she was itching to explore.

But could she do it?

No. Of course she couldn't.

She had collapsed onto the step and folded over and pressed her face into her hands. She felt awful for thinking of leaving her children, her home, her husband. But her feet wanted to run and run and never stop. She willed herself not to cry and managed to hold back any sobs. With eyes squeezed shut she just looked into the darkness of her own mind, searching for an answer. Elaine found herself asking the universe for someone with whom she could talk about the worries and strife she was experiencing – and, as luck would have it, the universe sent her exactly what she needed.

"Alrigh' there, lav?"

Elaine startled. She looked up to see the shadow of a gentleman standing over her. He looked to her like Santa Clause – if Santa Clause had grown up in South London and had never found a love of sweet treats and mince pies.

He was slender and had dark eyes, a thick white moustache and a full head of white hair to match. His face held wrinkles and lines from the years he had experienced, but they were not too heavy. His aura was light and playful and concerned. In his right hand he held a freshly lit cigarette, which he casually took a long drag from. He, thoughtfully, blew the smoke in a different direction.

"Good day, sir," She smiled, her best winning smile, despite her cheeks being stained. She wiped her face with the palm of her hand. She wanted to disguise the wet streaks that had squeezed through her tightly shut eyelids.

"None of that now," He frowned, "What's 'appened?"

Elaine noticed how, normally, someone would have asked if she was okay. This gentleman had skipped that question – as he had noticed, she guessed, that everything was *not* okay. He did not want to dilly-dally around that.

Elaine found herself briefly glancing behind her at the house. She was glad to notice that she could not see Robert – in either the kitchen, or behind any of the windows that faced the direction she was sat in. She quickly stood, moved into the alley, and closed the gate behind her, without locking it. She noticed how the man was the same height as she was. She suddenly felt very strange for being so quick to trust a stranger. Regardless, she found she was speaking before she even realised what she was saying.

"Just an argument," Elaine said, dismissive. Then: "...another argument."

"Marriage troubles, ey?"

"…You could say, I suppose, yes."

He took a long drag of his cigarette again and nodded, "He bein' a cant?"

The bluntness of the question took her by surprise, and she scoffed an unexpected laugh. It rippled out of her throat before she could stop it. If her mother had been there, she would have been dismayed by the use of language – and Elaine felt she should be, too. However, amazingly, she wasn't. Instead, it felt like a beautiful release to be able to smile. It was a wide and brilliant smile. She had not smiled like that in some time.

"Somewhat," She laughed, "How did you know?"

"He's a bloke, ain't he?" His grin was cheeky, fatherly.

She laughed again and it slowly faded as the reality of life settled in, and the novelty of the strange man's language began to wear off.

"Listen, darlin'," He said, finishing his cigarette and extinguishing it under his foot on the alley floor, "I'm no expert – don't claim to be – but if it means anythin' to you, there's always a way to fix samfin'. If he's being a twat, he'll come 'round. He'll apologise."

"Yes…" She said, sadly, "I thought so, too."

He appeared to know what she was getting at with that comment: "If he's not treatin' you right, lav," he went on, "You're allowed to leave – y'know that, right?"

Elaine shook her head, "It's not that simple, I'm afraid."

"Sure, it is! There's a dense wood on the other side of that field over there –" He said, pointing "– just been down there for a bit of a walk and explore. You can walk out of here now, if you wanted. Naffin stoppin' yer other than what's in your own head. Anyone can disappear incredibly quickly if they wanted to."

"As I said, it's not that simple," She repeated, "If I leave, I leave them with *him*."

"Ah. Little'ns?"

She nodded. He did the same, looking upwards at the sky.

"That is a tricky situation then miss, I must admit."

"I know…it's been awful. And I don't feel like if I told anybody about the awful things he does, that anybody would believe me."

"And why's that?"

"Because he's…reputable. He's good at the work he does, he's excellent friends with his colleagues and even my own parents sometimes appear to love him more than they love me…I just don't think anybody would be able to see the version of him that I see."

"Well I never even fackin' met him 'n' I already think he's a bastard," He said, matter-of-factly, "You can tell me what he gets up to, if you like."

Elaine thought for a long moment about whether or not that was something she wanted to do. This man was a stranger whom she'd never met, never seen before. Could she divulge to him the horrid things her husband did and said to her? Would he believe her? Would it, in some way, get back to Robert? Would she ruin her marriage by trusting in a stranger?

She heaved a heavy sigh as she realised: her perfect marriage had been ruined for some time already, and it most certainly was not due to her own hand.

Seeing her hesitation, the man said: "Think about it, lav. I spend most of my mornin's down the park, not far from here. If ever you wanted to find me again, 'ave a chat, you can find me there. Problem shared is a problem 'alved 'n' all that."

"Thank you," She said, "what was your name again?"

"Mickey," He answered.

"I'm Elaine."

"Nice to meet ya," He said, and nodded his head, in somewhat of a bow. Elaine knew that if he had been wearing a hat, he would have tipped it for her.

And with that, he disappeared down the alley, and into the town.

Elaine sat for some time on that step afterwards, somewhat bewildered by the whole experience. She sat and thought of the stranger and thought of his words, and the kind way in which he spoke to her. He was nice, and warm-hearted. It had been so long since anybody had spoken to her in that way. And, although she had only just met him, and did not know him in the slightest, Elaine was certain that this "Mickey" was the closest thing to a friend that she had, at that present moment.

It was *so nice* to have a friend.

CHAPTER 24

Mickey sat in the jail cell at the police station. His aging wrists felt sore from where the heavy metal cuffs had been gripping them. He absent-mindedly rubbed the liver-spotted skin, as he stared through the bars.

Custody was a loud and stressful place. Mickey did not remember it being so noisy and difficult– but then again, he thought, the only other previous occasion in which he had been arrested, he had been badly beaten, and had very little memory of the event at all.

The other people that he could see were far younger than he. Mickey was shocked to discover that most of them appeared to be just children. Each of them had the same pale and waxy, erratic look about them that Mickey remembered his brother Felix had had in his eyes, back when he was a teenager. High on drugs and lack of sleep. All the people surrounding him were thirty years or less, despite looking like standing-up skeletons, and almost every single one of them was male.

The females were sat in a separate jail cell opposite his own. There was three of them. Each of them stood as far away from one another as they possibly could. One of them hung onto the tiny window with the bars and tried to get the attention of the officers going past. One was lay face-down with an arm obscuring her face, trying to sleep. The third sat in the corner, curled with her knees against her chest, sobbing horrifically.

The men were making far more of a racket. One was just repeatedly banging his fist against the wall – a dull, awful, tedious rhythm that made Mickey long for some sort of change in pace, or some kind of melody to go alongside it. Another was yelling abuse through the tiny window at the officers that had arrested him. The officers were shouting back at him to get back into his cell and to keep quiet. One man was insistent that he was in pain and was clutching his wrist and groaning. Another man was watching the females in the opposite cell, and the female officers that were walking past, leering at them, jeering awfully crude remarks. Mickey sat on a metal bench, one which was bolted very firmly to the wall. The coldness of the metal sucking the warmth from his butt cheeks. He folded his arms across his chest and tried his best to find a way to sleep. This was made even more impossible when a new prisoner was brought into custody, making more noise than Mickey thought a single man capable of doing. Three very broad, very evidently strong officers practically carried him in. He thrashed about and threw his limbs in all directions, and yelled abuse at each of the police officers in turn. His aggression was not personal, nor particularly hurtful. It was just loud and annoying and disruptive. Mickey sighed. It was like being in a nursey school classroom. Except rather than three-year-old fighting over crayons, it was grown-ass-men fighting against the law, and authority.

Mickey didn't have the energy for any of that. He didn't see the point. He slouched further against the wall and shrugged his shoulders up, delving his hands deep into his pockets. He zipped up his fleece jacket, so it covered his chin, and closed his eyes. It wasn't the perfect place to sleep, but whilst people were wasting his time, he saw no point in trying to fight them and protest. He relinquished all power, he rested his eyes, he thought of why on earth he could be here, and napped.

CHAPTER 25

Elaine had thought about not doing it but had ended up giving into curiosity.

She had made her excuses and managed to get the neighbour to come over to babysit, just for an hour or so, while Elaine went out of the house. When asked where she was going, Elaine said she needed to nip into town just to run a few errands. Thankfully, the neighbour had not cared enough to ask for any more specifics. Christopher had quickly distracted her with a drawing of her he had done.

Elaine had grabbed her shopping bag and her purse – to keep up the charade – and headed out of the house and down the street. It was a reasonably sunny morning. The type of day where, to begin with, you presume you don't need a coat as the world is well-lit with a golden glow. But then a cool breeze ruffles the hem of your dress and suddenly there's goose-bumps all over your arms. This was what Elaine experienced, after all.

Regardless, she did not turn back to grab a cardigan, not wanting to waste a moment. She wasn't sure how long Mickey spent in the park, or if he would be there at all. On the off chance that he was, she didn't want to keep him waiting.

Her quickened pace meant that the walk to the park did not take her long. Elaine questioned herself with every fast-paced step she took, wondering why on earth was she agreeing to meet a strange old man in the park on a cool summer morning? It was quite possibly the strangest thing she had ever done. And yet, despite her dismay at her own actions, she did not allow herself to turn around or to hesitate.

It had been a week since she had first met Mickey in the alleyway. And he had been on her mind ever since. It was annoying sort of thought. The type similar to when a song is stuck in one's head, but only the same few lines are repeated on a loop. The only way to get rid of an earworm such as that was to listen to the song in full – or, in this case – meet the man again, intentionally, and clear her head.

And that was what she did.

She approached him from behind. There he was – sat on a bench along the path, wearing his black fleece jacket and smoking a cigarette. He was relaxed. His left ankle resting on his right knee, his arms outstretched along the back of the bench; the elbow of his right arm only bending for him to breathe in the sweet smokiness. Elaine paused – for just a second – before nodding to herself. She pushed on.

"Good morning, Mickey," she said.

He looked up at her, not in the slightest bit startled. When he spoke to her, he did so as if they had been friends for some years, "Good mornin' Elaine, my lav. How're you today?"

She found herself trying to smile, despite it being the last thing she really wanted to do. His face was gentle, kind, thoughtful. Patient.

"Curious," she answered. He waited, calmly, for her to explain, "Why does an older gentleman such as yourself want to hear about the silly troubles of a woman like me?"

He frowned, "Why d'you call 'em 'silly'?"

She shook her head, flustered, and shifted on the spot slightly. Her feet wanted to pace, but she forced herself to stand still. The indecision of it all made her go onto her tip-toes briefly and then back down again, "Because."

He raised his eyebrows.

"*Because!*" she was flustered, "That's what I've always been told: that I shouldn't be upset, that I'm being ever so silly, that

I should be grateful for the things I have and I should be happier with my lot in life..." her voice trailed off.

"Are you 'appy, though?"

In that moment, just by asking such a simple, innocent question, Elaine felt herself dwindle to the child she used to be. So innocent and full of hopes and dreams. The little girl she used to be whispered that this was not the life that she had always dreamed of – *this is not how it was supposed to go.*

Elaine slumped down and sat heavily on the bench. Her fingers gripped the edge of the seat tightly, and her bottom lip stuck out without her permission, "No," she answered, feebly, "No, I'm not happy."

"Well, I'm 'ere to listen," Mickey answered, "If that's what you want me to do. I'm not offended if that's not the case. But I have naffin' else to do today. And, correct me if I'm wrong, but I think when a woman is found cryin' on her own doorstep, afraid that someone will see her talking to a stranger, that there is something very, very wrong."

Her gaze was sad as she looked down at the grass. It was a vibrant green. The birds tweeted above her. The day would have otherwise been especially lovely if it weren't for the topic of conversation that she was trying so hard to dig out of herself.

"You're right," She said, "Of course you are right."

"I will listen," He said, gently, "Tell it all."

And then she had taken a deep breath and told him everything. It was an hour that passed by quicker than she realised, and the words at first came out in dips, infrequently, in unexpected little bursts. She didn't know how to do it, how to talk. But Mickey showed her the art of conversation. He coaxed from her the courage to speak of the things she had been wishing for so long to discuss with someone, anyone. Together, they found her words, buried deep inside her gut – twisted and confused and covered by feelings of guilt and sadness and manipulation. Elaine and Mickey uncovered them together and took them out and laid them on the grass, and amongst the leaves in the trees. They looked at them and they analysed them, and at no point did Elaine feel like what she had said was shocking, or awful, or irregular. At no point did she feel judged, or unsafe. This was what amazed Elaine the most. She had forgotten that people could be kind. It had been so long since she had sat and spoken about how she felt. She had forgotten how to talk about herself and her sadness. Amazingly though, once it was out, the sadness and the ideas weren't as scary as she originally thought them to be.

"What do you think I should do?" She found herself asking, desperately. She had cried so much, soft tears and shaky breaths, and had ended up laughing at herself. She had cried so often lately. Where did all these tears even come from?

"I can't make that decision for you, lav," He said quietly, "You know as well as I do that, no matter what 'appens, you have to be the one to call the shots."

Elaine nodded in agreement, "Of course." She said.

"One fing I will advise though...'im layin' his 'ands on you ain't okay. You need to get yourself a back-up in case he goes crazy 'n'...*really* tries to hurt yer, if yer catch me drift."

"Like what?" She said, exasperated, and laughed again, "A gun?"

Mickey looked back at her and didn't blink. She couldn't pinpoint his emotion, but it most certainly was not laughter. He was not joking at her suggestion. Her laughter faded quickly.

"You're not serious?" She scoffed, "A gun? Mickey, where would I get a *gun*?"

He shrugged, nonchalant, then stifled a yawn.

"Look," he said, "I know this is all very strange. I know you 'ave no reason to listen to me. But I believe in followin' me gut. And me gut told me to look after you. You're a good person, Elaine, 'n' it saddens me that this bloke of yours won't recognise that. I don't know you, I don't know your last name, I don't know the name of this twat that you confess to being in love with – and I'm not suggestin' you murder him or anything like that, but...by the sounds of it, sometimes, he's a nasty piece of work. And you 'n' your kids shouldn't have to deal with that.

What worries me…is that if he's done all the things you've told me about – the manipulation, throwin' the table, forcin' you to do fings you don't want to…where does he draw the line? If at all?"

There was a long silence as his words sank in. Elaine looked at him with wide, frightened eyes. As much as she hated to listen, she couldn't help it – she knew it was all right, all a possibility.

"He'd kill me, if he wanted to," She said. She was certain of it, "I don't think he'd give it a second thought."

"I fink you're right there," Mickey answered, "I don't fink he'd stop either. So…if you want protection, I can get you protection. Just in case the worst should 'appen, 'n' he goes for you…better safe than sorry."

They had met several times after this. The next time Mickey had asked her how things were, and she had said things were better – he was trying, he was buying her flowers and cleaning the dishes. But the time after that, Robert had been awful to her again and held her hand under a scalding tap because the tea she had made him hadn't been hot enough. He wanted to check she knew what the correct temperature was, and that she wouldn't forget it. It was at this point when Mickey had brought forward from the inside pocket of his coat: a pistol.

Elaine had recoiled at first, terrified of seeing a real gun: a real-life, heavy, silver, loaded gun. But Mickey had explained how it worked, and she quickly calmed down. The times after that, he took her to fields and woodland where she could practice how to shoot.

"Yer don't need to be an expert," he said to her, "You just need to be confident enough to pull the trigger, should you need to."

She hadn't enjoyed it at first, but, to her amazement, the more she tried, the more empowered she felt. Elaine began to thoroughly enjoy her weekly, to bi-weekly meetings with Mickey and the time they shared together. She learned about his childhood, and about his mother, and about how he had spent a few years as a lorry driver and had travelled around Africa. Elaine was fascinated to hear about his life, despite the modesty with which he shared his stories. For a confident man, she thought, he wasn't half shy.

"Thank you for this, Mickey," She had said one afternoon, as they walked the walk back to the park, where they always parted ways – he never once walked with her to her house, "I haven't had a friend in a very long time. It's always so nice to see you. Thank you for listening so well."

"Pfft," he brushed it off, shrugged, "Don't be silly. It's been no trouble."

Mickey brought out his packet of cigarettes and his lighter and lit one up. He, too, had enjoyed the time they had spent together. He had not tutored and encouraged someone in such a way as this since he had first met Marcus. It was strange, but comfortable. Spending time with Elaine, he thought, was almost like having a grown-up daughter of his own. Perhaps that was what she was, in a different life. He felt his advice was really not valid, as he had never been in her situation. But in his heart, he knew that Elaine was worthy of safety and protection. He knew that it was by no fault of her own that she had ended up in such an awful situation. He was grateful that she, too, had been enjoying their time together just as much. Two lonely, lost souls, bonding over sadness.

"Good afternoon, Mickey," she said, waving goodbye at the end of the street.

"Call me Mouse, lav," He said.

They shared an awkward wave and a small smile, and parted ways once more.

CHAPTER 26

As a young man, Mickey had not enjoyed his time in prison. It was loud, it was crowded, it was dark and gritty and corrupted. Nobody visited him. Not even his own mother. Mickey began to question as to whether his mum even knew where he was...

Despite not fitting in as one of the stereotypical prisoners, Mickey only took a few months to settle in before his prison mates left him be. They had said that the newbies needed to earn their right to be accepted within the community. Mickey had outright refused to do anything that was asked of him. No, he was not going to cause a distraction so they could smuggle drugs. No, he was not going to beat up the biggest guy in the place for no reason. No, he was not going to give them the rest of his lunch.

"This ain't school," He said to them, calmly, "I ain't givin' yer any of ma dinner money, if that's what you're after."

They'd tried to ambush him. Tried to catch him off guard and teach him a lesson with their fists – and, to be honest, they did connect with a few of their right-hooks. However, the inmates were baffled by the raw animalistic side of Mickey that came out when he was attacked. Still, he remained so calm. But the friendly approachable nature by which he had become well-known was quickly snapped away. In its place stood a cold and unforgiving figure who got what he wanted. And what Mickey wanted were two-fold:

He wanted to get out as soon as possible.

And he wanted to be left alone.

A few teeth and bones had to be broken before the rest of the prison inmates thoroughly learned this lesson. But Mickey soon became notorious for his cold, calm, collected stare. Anybody who dared look at him wrong? His beady eyes would follow them around the yard for the rest of that afternoon.

He was twenty-six years old when he was finally released; early, due to good behaviour. For Mickey, the seven years that had passed were the most bizarre of his life. Despite dragging at the time, despite feeling like he really was going to be in that tiny grey room for the rest of his days. When he stood there, alone, with his few belongings in front of the prison gates, he felt like he had only blinked since he had first walked through them. He had entered that building as a boy, and now he was a man – and had, amazingly, missed that transition entirely.

The first thing Mickey did was try to find his mother. Seven years – would she remember him? Would she recognise him? Would she even want to *see* him?

Mickey had pondered the many reasons why she hadn't come to visit him. Perhaps she was ashamed of him and had told everybody that he had gone working abroad, ignoring the problem. Perhaps she was unsure of whether or not he was the son she thought he was – did she believe that he really did those things he was convicted of? Mickey was angry at Felix for leaving him that evening...but, then again, maybe Felix was unaware of what had happened. Maybe Felix had been out there looking for him all these years, trying to find him and help him? For all he knew, Mickey could have simply run away. He had left Mickey on a street corner one evening, and when he returned, he was gone. Was he to know that those men would approach and mistake his identity? Was he to know that he would be taken away by the police? Mickey had no way of knowing.

His feet, out of memory, took him on the long journey to his mother's front door. There was a train and several buses, and a very long walk involved.

Maybe that was why she never visited – she couldn't find the place or couldn't afford to. Did she even know that was where he had been? Had anybody told her? Had it been in the news? Maybe she thought he had run away as well.

It was such a bizarre feeling, standing on the same street, looking at the same front door. Mickey couldn't bring it within himself to place a foot on the pathway. It looked exactly the same as it had done before. But there was a set of net curtains up in the front room now, obscuring the view of the room from anybody passing by the street. His mother had always said she wanted to do that...

Regardless, he picked up his feet and he walked the four paces to the front door. He had his house key with him, but it somehow felt wrong to use it. He hadn't lived in the house for almost a decade. What if his mother didn't even recognise him? The last thing he wanted to do would be to give her a fright.

Mickey tightened and flexed his hands. They were fidgety. They wanted to knock whilst simultaneously wanting to not-knock. Those hands had done worst things whilst behind prison walls than they had done before he had been wrongly sent into the stony building...Funny, that.

He raised his knuckles and rapped. A slow, hesitant, ashamed *rap-tat-tat*.

He waited.

There was noise coming from within the house. The sound of a little girl squealing in delight as she played with her toys, all too excitedly. The sound of cupboard doors banging shut as they were closed a little too quickly. Footsteps, heading up the hallway.

The door was unlocked, unchained, unbolted, and opened...

But it was not his mother on the other side of it.

"Can I help you?" a lady said, impatiently. She had brown-ginger hair and a bright green blouse on, with beige slacks. Her hair was tied up on the top of her head with a deep blue silk scarf. Her cigarette was balanced on her lip as she spoke.

Mickey blinked, hard. He felt confused, "I'm looking for Molly Donaldson?"

The woman shook her head, "Sorry – she's not lived here in years." She went to close the door again, but Mickey held out a firm hand to stop it. He kept his eyes on the woman through the small gap in the door.

"Please," He begged, "Do you know where I can find her?"

There was a very long pause where neither of them moved, nor spoke. Then, her expression softened: "Bramcote Road," She answered, "You'll find her there. She's by the apple tree."

The door closed. And it did not reopen.

The more Mickey walked the more Bramcote Road appeared to be familiar to him. He wasn't exactly sure of its whereabouts, so asked a local shopkeeper, who was more than happy to assist with directions. It wasn't too far; about a forty-minute walk.

And then he saw her. By the apple tree, just as the lady with the ginger hair had told him. In the centre of a field, surrounded by slabs of rock, in varying shades of black and grey, various varieties of shiny or matte.

"Hi, mum," He said.

She did not answer him. Mickey could not see her face, after all. When he thought about it, he guessed he really didn't want to, either.

The tombstone read: *Molly Jane Donaldson, mother and friend to all.* Followed by the dates of her birth and death. What hurt Mickey the most was realising she had died five years ago – he had been in prison for two years. The past five he had lived, unknowingly, without a mum.

He knelt on the grass and looked at the headstone. It was entirely undecorated. Bare and plain, nothing special about it. Mickey wondered who had made the arrangements for her. He wondered how it had happened, and why. He wondered if Felix knew any of the answers – if he knew that their mother was dead at all.

Mickey kissed his fingertips, then placed them gently on the top of the headstone and closed his eyes, for a small, private moment. Then, he headed out of Bramcote Cemetery, with one mission and one mission only:

To find his brother.

CHAPTER 27

Marcus had decided he had had enough of all the mysteries, all the fun and games, all the lies and all the deceit. Mickey was his friend – or, was supposed to be, anyways. If he had a car, a twin brother, a split personality, even a fucking black hole parallel-universe dumb sci-fi shit – Marcus wanted to know about it.

He was in such a rage, his arms crossed firmly over his chest to brace form the cold, his fists clenched and aching from the frosty air. He felt so betrayed that Mickey had been keeping something from him – or that, at the garage, he had pretended to hardly know him. Whichever the case, he was not happy. He wanted to know who Felix was. He wanted to know why he hadn't been told about him before. He wanted to know why Felix hadn't made an appearance – until now.

He stomped through the park on the way to Mickey's set of flats. The grass was littered with a glistening sheen of frost, and Marcus could see his breathing as he walked. He stared at nothing in front of him – only the path beneath his feet as he put one loud and annoyed foot in front of the other.

It was this lack of awareness that led to Marcus bumping into somebody. He had been totally oblivious to anybody else being around and, as luck would have it, the only other person in the whole park who was about that time of morning, was a young woman, walking alone, on the way to the post office.

She, too, was not entirely conscious of where her direction was taking her in. Hence why the two of them clattered into one another and toppled to the ground.

"Watch where you're –" Marcus began to say, his grumpy mood showing more than just a little around the edges. But then he looked up and noticed the lady, entirely dressed in black, her blonde curls hanging around her face, her cheeks and the tip of her nose pink from the cold.

"I'm terribly sorry," She muttered, breathless. She said the words into a fluffy black scarf that was wrapped loosely around her neck.

The two of them got to their feet.

"No, no, it's okay" Marcus said. He thought for a second, and remembered when Mickey had told him the story of the night at the theatre; where the man had been rude to him after finding his wallet, "Wait, you're...Elaine, right?"

She nodded, then paused, "Why is that important?"

"My friend Mickey works at the theatre and saw you and your husband before the...before it happened," He answered, "I just recognised you from his description. I didn't realise the two of you lived so close."

She smiled, kindly, "Mickey as in Mouse?" she asked.

Marcus tried to maintain an expression that showed only mild curiosity, rather than the overwhelming feeling of exasperation that he was truly feeling.

"Oh, so you know him well?"

"Yes, Mouse and I are quite good friends, in fact." She answered, "I haven't seen him in a while, though. But we used to meet every week."

"I never knew this, he never told me," Marcus chuckled a soft, tired laugh, "Every week?"

"Yes, he was ever so kind to me. I'm very grateful for everything he did."

"What did he do?"

"Well..." She took a very long pause and seemed to eye Marcus up and down, as if she was trying to figure out if she could trust him. Elaine decided that a friend of Mickey's was a friend of her own, "Well, my husband was not a very nice man; not all the time, anyway." She fiddled with a button on her coat sleeve, "Mouse and I talked at great length of the difficulties I was having. His listening ear allowed me to make the decision to leave my husband."

"To leave him?"

"Well, that was the plan..." Elaine said, drifting off, "Until this happened, of course. This was not what I had planned for at all."

Her eyes got teary and suddenly Marcus felt incredibly awkward as he stood with a lady he had never met before, but only heard of through his friend's stories, or in the newspaper.

"I'm sorry," She breathed, and pressed a hand to her mouth, delicately, "It's still quite a shock to talk about, y'know? I just can't believe it happened. It's dreadful."

She allowed a few small tears to escape before looking upwards and trying to blink them away.

"I'm sorry, I'm sorry," She said again, and her little pink nose sniffed in the cold air, "I'll let you be on your way. I have places to be myself." She gently patted him on the arm, "If you see Mouse, tell him to come and visit, won't you? I don't have his telephone number."

Marcus watched her go. He was bewildered by all the information he had received in such a short amount of time. Without hesitation, he collected his wits and shoved his hands deep into his pockets and continued the brisk walk to Mickey's set of flats. He nodded to the doorman as he rushed past and climbed the three sets of stairs that were needed to take him to the front door of the flat.

When he got to it, he knocked and knocked and knocked.

No answer.

Nobody was home.

CHAPTER 28

Robert Brooker sat in the driver's seat of his car, the head of a young attractive woman between his thighs.

God, he thought, *this is the life...*

He had driven the two of them to a secluded country road, so it made no difference that it was broad daylight. It was chilly, but he had the in-built car heaters on. The windows were beginning to get a little steamy.

The young woman was someone who worked in his set of offices. They had been flirtatious for some time, and it was today that he had suggested they go for lunch and a long drive. It was simply by mild suggestion that he managed to get her to agree to the long drive first. After that, it was easy to get her to unzip his trousers and do whatever he asked of her. She was very eager to please.

Brooker knew he would let this continue until they had to return to the office – and when he did so, he'd make sure to mention they no longer had time to get lunch. That way he didn't have to fork out for a meal that he didn't want to pay for – and nobody in town would see him eating with a woman that was not his wife.

Although, he thought, that problem would soon be swept under the rug. As great as Elaine was at looking after the house and the children, and yes, she was pretty, she was just a bit...boring to him now. She didn't do anything for him. And neither did that hideous brown cardigan she wore around the house when it was chilly. She never made an effort. She really ought to get rid of that horrid oversized thing.

"But my dad bought it for me," She protested, when he had told her his thoughts on her fashion choices, "And I only wear it around the house."

"You should make more of an effort for me. There are so many days when you don't wear a pretty dress, or you don't put on any make up. It's quite sad, really. It doesn't *do* anything for me. Also – you *really* ought to start plucking your eyebrows more often, don't you think?"

He hadn't said any of it to be hurtful. She was always saying how communication and openness and honesty were very important in a marriage. He was simply doing what she wanted him to do. He was being open and honest. And, honestly, the cardigan made her look like a fifty-year-old washer woman from the 1700s.

He sighed. Still, she would not be around much longer. He had that to be thankful for. The guy he had spoken to drove a tough deal, but they had eventually found a number they would agree on. Robert figured that once Elaine was dead, he would inherit any money she had squirrelled away from him, anyway (he *knew* she had separate bank accounts to him, he'd seen the letters in the post...silly woman). So, effectively, she was paying for it herself. How charming of her.

He had thought long and hard about murdering her himself, many times. It would be so easy. She was so puny, and he knew that she wouldn't fight back – she loved him. She said it over and over every day, in every tone of voice, when she felt any kind of emotion. Especially when she was scared or upset. It was *ever* so annoying. He could easily stab her repeatedly in the stomach when she lay asleep, in bed; or he could lock her away in a room for several weeks until he could no longer hear her whimpers; or he could set the house on fire with her still in it; or choke her to death in the kitchen with his bare hands...so many brilliant options to choose from. But Brooker was a man who prided himself on cleanliness – his entire aesthetic was clean-cut, clean-shaven, clean suit, clean, dazzling smile. And, in all honesty, he thought he would simply enjoy himself far too much and end up botching it in some way – either not completing his task efficiently enough or leaving a trail of evidence in which the finger pointed plainly at him. Robert was having none of that. He wanted rid of his wife, and so he would do so privately, quietly, and cleanly – by a professional, unrelated to them both, who knew what he was doing.

Brooker had spoken to the man named Felix and been very clear – he did not care how it was done, but he was adamant that it must not hold him, in any way, a suspect. He wanted to be out of the way, come home and *oh no, my wife appears to be dead, goodness me, how did that ever happen? Silly Elaine.*

Felix had agreed to the terms, enlightened by the creativity. Robert was sure he was robbing him blind but was new to this kind of thing, so paid the man what he demanded, after only a small amount of bartering.

Soon she'd be dead, what did it matter?

He grabbed the hair of the young woman that was pleasuring him and pushed her head down further, so she made a horrendous gagging sound. He smirked, tilted his own head back, and relaxed.

What a great life, he thought.

What a great life indeed.

CHAPTER 29

Felix sat alone in the pub, sipping from the tumbler, filled with the usual liquor of choice and a single ice cube, this time. He took a long drag on his cigarette, blowing the smoke into the air gently, watching it morph and change with the airflow.

The pub was hot and humid, and he'd rolled up his shirt sleeves to his elbows. Far too hot to be wearing his leather jacket in there that evening. It was a Friday, and although outside was cold, the windows of the pub were entirely steamed up and the many bodies inside were more than comfortably warm.

Felix had placed a pound coin on the edge of the pool table to indicate he was next in line. When he had approached, the men playing had looked like they were somewhat threatened by his stance. Felix was amused by this. He was even more amused by how they relaxed when he simply placed the coin down and walked away again.

The warmth of the whisky wasn't doing it for him this evening. He was glad of the single ice cube. He looked at the perfectly polished taps which the lagers were poured from. They were the drink of choice for most of the young gents in the building that night…Felix was not really one to drink cheap – but they did look refreshing.

"I thought I'd find you here."

Sat on his stool, Felix swivelled around to see who was

speaking to him. They had done well to sneak up on him – he was normally not someone who could be too surprised, especially in his local.

"Mouse," He nodded, "drink?"

"No." He said, dismissing the offer as quick as extinguishing a candle with bare fingertips, "I need to talk to you. Outside."

"You *need* to?"

"Outside, Fred. Now."

Felix widened his eyes at being called by his real name. It had been a good long time since somebody had called him that. It was only his brother that could do so, the only person who really *knew* his real name – and it had a bewitching effect on him. Felix was calm, collected, cool. Fred was erratic, nervous, timid – Fred was still seven years old.

It caused a moment of weakness. Felix stood and followed his brother out of the back door of the pub, bringing his drink with him. Mickey noticed the sheltered area under which a few others were smoking – the ones that preferred to do so outside, to get some fresh air – and decided he needed more privacy. He grabbed hold of Felix's elbow and strode onto the grassy area. A selection of park benches were littered around in the dark, absent from their use in the winter months. Felix protested at being man-handled, but Mickey ignored him.

He swung him around to face him, satisfied that they were in a place where they could not be overheard.

"Well?" Felix said.

"This job you were on about," He said, "Who was it? What was 'er name?"

"Oh, so you're interested now?" Felix tried to be cocky but was quickly cut short by Mickey's growled response.

"Enough of the fackin' games! Tell me!"

"It was a man called Robert Brooker who approached me, he's the one paying me," Felix said, "he wants his wife killed."

"An' his wife is called...?"

"Elaine."

This news appeared to affect his brother. His top lip looked as if it wanted to curl into a snarl, but he kept it under control. His entire face twisted as if he smelled something putrid.

"I thought so." He said.

"Why, what's the problem?"

"I know her. That's the problem. And Robert Brooker is a fackin' *cant*." He spat onto the grass, "A *coward* is what 'e is!"

Felix withdrew slightly but made it as apparent as he could that he was not intimidated by his brother – even if that was, not strictly, true.

"You can't give 'im what 'e wants, Fred."

"Why not? It's a job. It's *my* job."

"I don't fackin' care. If you've got any heart, you won't do it."

Felix stood for a moment, feeling like a schoolboy being told off for not doing his homework, "You don't tell me what to do." He hissed.

"Funny that, 'cause I'm pretty sure I just fackin' *did*."

"You want me to just give up a job, as easy as this? He's paying me *hundreds* for this."

Mickey took a large stride forward, so his face was inches away from Felix's. His eyes were dark and menacing, "You listen 'ere you fackin' little prick," He said quietly; a dark and sinister voice that was quietly spoken, but indescribably intimidating, "I've spoken to that girl. I know 'er, and I know 'er well. If you take 'er life, you'll have *me* to answer to."

Felix stared back. He did his best not to let his gaze drop to the ground, as much as it wanted to; "What's so great about her?"

"She's a good person. Her *husband* is a fackin' cant. He's the one that deserves to have his lights out." He lit a cigarette, took a drag, then spat on the grass, "Hope the miserable bastard rots in hell. Now promise me you won't do it," Mickey said, pointing a finger at his brother – the same hand that held the cigarette. It's glowing end littered ash over Felix's chest as he pointed. He couldn't help but withdraw.

He nodded. "Promise."

"Good." He started to walk back over the grass, toward the road, on his walk home. He didn't look back when he next spoke, but he was sure to say it loud enough so that Felix could hear him; "See to it that it ain't broken – or I'll break your fackin' face."

CHAPTER 30

Olwyn busied herself in the office at the theatre. She had an electric vacuum cleaner and was enjoying herself as she picked up the debris and dust that was littered across the forest-green carpet. It as old and beaten down, but she was not. Her spirits were high as she ensured to suck up every little piece of lint.

She often helped with the cleaning jobs, just to top up her hours a little bit. She was good at cleaning and, unlike the majority of people, quite enjoyed it. She was someone who *genuinely* found it therapeutic. Rather than just *claiming* it to be, in a moment of superior ego.

After a moment, she saw the file that she had been looking for. She often had a bit of a nosey when she was in the office – why not? If they wanted to keep important paperwork a secret, they shouldn't keep the office so messy, and leave things out on desks where they can easily be seen or swiped.

She picked up the rota and the time sheet from the previous week. It was all written out by hand in – *ah, wonderful* – pencil. They hadn't yet switched to these new "computers" that every business appeared to be getting nowadays. The theatre was an old-fashioned place and did things the way they always did – pen and paper. Or, typewriter, if they were being really formal.

Olwyn found a pencil amongst the mess of paperwork on

the desk. A yellow HB one, with a little pink rubber on the end. How perfect.

Next to the line where it read Michael Donaldson on the rota, she traced her finger across and found February 13th. It had listed that Mouse was on until nine o'clock. She rubbed it out. And instead wrote one o'clock, the following morning. She took out the time sheet and did the same for him.

There we go, she thought, *just as he asked.*

She then picked up the vacuum cleaner again, popped the pencil back in the pot, and busied herself on with her work.

CHAPTER 31

The interview room was brilliantly bright, but not in the way the movies depicted it.

It was not a dark room with one, single, bare light-bulb, used only for blinding people. No, it looked more like a bare classroom. And all the artificial lighting was white and bright and blinding. He concluded it was designed to keep any-body who was within, awake.

The two officers sat opposite him. They were not the ones who had arrested him at his home – they were instead two gentlemen, one whom was around Mickey's own age, the other some decades younger. The elder was balding and grey around the edges, with bright blue eyes and a concerned resting facial position. The younger of the two was tanned and tall and, to Mickey, looked as if he was just in the job for the glamour that came with the title.

"I told yer already," Mickey repeated, "It wasn't me. You've got the wrong man."

"When Robert Brooker did not pay you thanks for retriev-ing his wallet, how did you react?"

"I didn't. I've dealt with rude customers before. 'Im and his flashy sports car didn't bother me."

There was a long pause, and the older of the officers looked down at his notes. He nodded, thoughtful, then looked up.

"And what of your previous criminal history?"

Mickey blinked, "What of it?"

"According to your records, you have been convicted of murder before, some thirty years ago, for murder of a woman by the name of Sally Stinson."

"Yeah, I went to prison for seven years," Mickey clarified, "But I did not commit the crime."

"The evidence begs to differ - there were three eye-witnesses, all of whom looked at you in the stand at court and said that you were the one who did it."

"Well what I'm gonna bet ain't written in your file," Mickey answered calmly, leaning back in his chair, "is any mention of a man called Fredrick 'Felix' Donaldson."

The older officer calmly looked down at his papers again. The younger officer shifted in his chair, slightly uncomfortable.

"What of him?"

"He's my brother," Mickey said, "We're twins."

The older officer looked up, "Twins?"

"Twins. Identical."

"There's no record of you having a brother."

"That's because it was believed he drowned in a river when he was seven years old, along with another kid called Jon."

The older man looked thoughtful again and nodded, "I remember that story; the newspaper headlines went nationwide. They were both confirmed dead."

Mickey shook his head, "Fred's body was never found."

And then Mickey explained. He was there for some time as he explained, in depth, the façade that the two of them had concocted when they were younger. He spoke of Fred's developing drug habit, and his brush with the law, and his withdrawal from the family home. He spoke of the night he had seen him, and how he had been beaten up something terrible, how he had been arrested and not believed – and how he had had no visitors when he had been sent to prison for seven years. He spoke of coming out of prison and finding his mother had passed, and then spending some months hunting down his brother 'Felix' to find some connection to his roots, to his family. He had moved up north so he could start a new life. Felix had followed him, and the two had met, on the very rare occasion, to catch up.

"You expect us to believe that?" The younger officer said, smirking. He shook his head in disbelief.

Mickey placed a piece of paper on the table. It was no bigger than a credit card. It had been written on in black sharpie, in slanted, harsh handwriting.

The older officer picked it up and looked at it as if it had something crude and offensive written on it; "What's this?" he asked, unimpressed.

Mickey crossed his arms across his chest. He was not flattered by the tone in which he was being spoken to but did his very best to keep his cool. He took a deep breath and kept his face neutral, emotionless, as he answered:

"His home address."

CHAPTER 32

"On my count," the officer whispered to his colleagues.

They had marched together up the slender rickety stairway, all dressed from head to toe in their heavy body armour – stab vests and shoulder pads and the few that carried the battering ram also had helmets and face shields.

The set of flats was dingy, dark and smelled of stale urine and cannabis. Babies could be heard crying through the walls, with arguments occurring. Any that were stood in the hallway quickly quietened when they saw the parade of police officers coming through. It was the dead of night, and yet the building was still very much wide awake. Trouble never sleeps. Not in this end of town, at least.

They stood outside the door they were looking for, quiet and strategic. Trained impeccably. The sergeant in the lead counted with his fingers; *three...two...one...*

They barged through the front door, wood and metal splintering everywhere across the tiny living space. The peace and quiet that had been created as they marched silently up the stairwell vanished, and the officers ran into the apartment, ready for battle, not caring what they shoved aside, nor what was trampled and broken in their path.

And then, again...stillness.

The officers stood frozen, defeated. The adrenaline still

ran through their veins and some stood breathing heavily or scratching their head just for something to do with the overflow of energy they had gained.

"Well..." One of them said, "He wasn't wrong."

"There's a note," Said another.

The sergeant walked forward and snatched the envelope out of his colleague's hand. It was not expensive paper; the envelope was perhaps the type you got for free with birthday cards that are less than fifty pence. The paper inside was thin, and cheap.

His handwriting was scratchy, but carefully written, and readable.

"It's all here," He said quietly, reading it, "Michael Donaldson was right. He did it. Fred, Felix, whatever his name is..."

"It's a confession?"

"Yes."

"Then what's with, uh..." The officer indicated to what the entire room were looking at.

"Guilt," Said the sergeant, "He's written here that his brother tried to talk him out of it. Couldn't bear to betray him again, blah-blah-blah." He sniffed, then grimaced, "Someone call the coroner."

The sergeant placed the letter in a clear plastic bag, sealed it shut, then gave his colleagues further instructions. The silence of the place was unsettlingly still. Like the noise after the last note of a song at a live concert – reverberating through the air, impacting the audience with a combination of impressiveness and a small amount of anticlimactic energy.

One by one, the extra officers left. Four remained, to protect the crime scene, to shun the nosey neighbours that were desperate to get in and have a look. All of them could not help but have their eyes continuously drawn to the sight in the centre of the room. They did not want to look, but the sight of it was captivating. Their brains demanded that they memorise every horrid detail.

Felix remained still and silent. He was wearing his flannel

shirt, untucked, and a pair of bright blue jeans. His shoes were strong, sturdy boots. They dangled in the air.

"Do I move this?" one of the officers asked, indicating to a chair that had fallen onto its back, near to Felix.

"No, leave the crime scene as it is. They'll want to take pictures of it and all that."

The officer nodded and moved away, being careful not to touch Felix as he walked past again.

Felix hung from the light fixture by a rope, his face and hands purple from the pooling of blood in his limbs and the lack of air in his chest. His eyes were part-open, part-closed, and the ghastly whites of his eyes had rolled back, making him appear possessed.

The case was closed: Felix had done it.

The coroners arrived and took him away.

CHAPTER 33

Now for what really happened.

Mickey did not bother to knock. He knew Felix did not lock his front door. In a neighbourhood like Felix's, it was perhaps equally safe to not and to do so – if someone wanted to get in, they were going to, either way. Felix was grateful he had a bit of a reputation, and loyal neighbours.

"You ready?" Mickey said.

"Yeah, gimme a sec!" He called from another room.

It was the night Felix was going to visit the Brooker household. Mickey had come along to ensure that Felix was still doing what he had said he was going to do – murder Robert, and not Elaine.

Felix emerged from his messy bedroom. His leather jacket swung over his shoulders. He threw a different t-shirt behind him, onto the bedroom floor. He wore a flannel shirt and blue jeans and boots on his feet – not exactly the assassin that Mickey was expecting. But whatever worked for him.

"You've got everything you need?" Mickey checked.

"Yeah, I believe so," Felix displayed under his jacket how he had one hand pistol tucked out of sight.

"You're killing him with *that*?"

"Don't sound so unimpressed," Felix said, with a smirk, "It's not all about size, y'know." He fidgeted with his collar and straightened it where it was itching his neck, "If in doubt though, always come prepared. I'm planning on using this..."

From his waistband, he lifted up his un-tucked shirt and brought out from his trouser leg a sawn-off shot gun.

"Fackin' 'ell Fred, you'll blow him to *pieces!*" Mouse laughed, which tapered off into a chuckle, "Brutal." He watched as Felix busied himself with counting bullets and ensuring both of the guns were clean. He sat down on his sofa and placed them both on the coffee table.

The place was quite a mess. Really the opposite of how Mickey kept his flat. There were bits and pieces littered all around the place. Empty crisp packets and plastic bags just thrown on the floor when their purpose was fulfilled. There was a single dying plant on the windowsill, which Mickey guessed had not been watered that year. There was a reel of rope beside the coffee table, with pieces of cars next to it: exhausts and alloys and engine cogs. On the wall – the only part of the room that appeared to have any pride in it – was a beautiful display of Felix's gun collection. There were rifles and revolvers and pistols and even a submachine gun. The oddest of which was probably a crossbow, that hung directly in the centre of the messy masterpiece. Each of them had their own space on the wall, displayed and polished in all their glory. Mickey thought it a very stupid thing to have a wall of easily-accessible weapons in a room that was not the bedroom, and then an unlocked front door. But he did not tell his brother how to live his day-to-day life – even if he did live in something similar to a junk yard.

"Do you know where he's going to be?"

"Yes." Felix answered. He did not expand on his answer.

"And you know how you're going to do it?"

"Do what?"

Mickey raised a confused eyebrow, "Kill him?"

Felix took a deep inhale through his nose and placed his shot gun on the coffee table again, "About that, Mouse..."

Mickey froze. He turned around sharply from where he had been admiring the museum of killing machines, "*What* about it?" he hissed.

Felix cleared his throat, "I've been thinking about it, about what you said, and…"

"And you're backing out?"

"Well, no, but…I need money, Mouse. I need money *bad*."

Mickey shook his head in disbelief, "This is happening all over again. Thirty years ago, you did the exact same to me. You wanted money, you facked it up, you threw me under the fackin bus. Ain't that right?"

Felix didn't answer.

"You're a fackin' *coward* you are," He spat, "You want money more than you want real justice?"

"I need to *live*, Mouse!"

Mickey shook his head in disbelief, "You embarrass me."

"I need the money," He repeated, "I don't care what you say. I'm going to kill the wife."

Mickey scowled, his eyebrows furrowing lowered than Felix had ever seen them go, "No you're fackin' not."

"There's no money in killing the husband – he's the one that's bloody *paying* me!"

"You don't get it, do you?" Mickey had raised his voice now, and was shouting right into his brother's face, "You just don't have any fackin conscious! She's not *done* anything, *he's* the one that's a fackin psychopath, throwing bleedin' dining tables at her, and raping 'er in their own martial bed. You want to be a fackin' hero Fred, then why not start *acting* like one? She's a fackin' *mother* for Pete's sakes!"

"Oh, who *cares* if she's made a couple of rug-rats?" He threw back, "I never gave a fuck about our *own* mother. You think I'm gonna care about some fuckin' stranger and her kids? Am I *fuck!*"

Mickey stood for a second, his heart pumping, his eyes filled with rage, "Don't speak ill of the dead," He hissed. He could feel the anger building in his brain. There was something similar to a rubber band. It was tightening and tightening with every word that Felix uttered.

"Oh, shut the fuck up, Mouse," Felix went on. He, too, was

noticeably angry. Fearless and agitated, "I didn't care about her – I didn't. I spent years watching from the outside how fucking *over dramatic* she was, and I was sick of it. As soon as you went to prison, I moved back in pretending to be you and I robbed her of everything she fuckin' had. The reason she fuckin passed away was probably 'cause she thought her fuckin golden boy had turned nasty and she couldn't cope with it. I didn't go to the funeral. I just left her there until the neighbours found her. So, don't try and use the *she's a mother* argument on me, because that doesn't entitle someone to *anything!*"

Ping. There it was. The rubber band had snapped. Everything about Mickey's time in prison all just clicked into place, and he suddenly couldn't contain his rage anymore. His vision went red, and his blood boiled in his veins. He lunged for him, across the coffee table, and grabbed him by the collar.

Felix was quick to react and the two struggled and fought. They spat insults at one another as they wrestled. Mickey planted a foot in his brother's stomach and kneed him between the legs. Felix swung an elbow towards Mickey's face, but it missed – just.

Mickey wasn't there for words. There were no more words left to be said. He had heard all he needed to hear. Felix was not going to change his ways and reach towards what was good. He was not going to grasp the opportunity to do the right thing, and *not* kill the wrong person. Mickey was having none of it.

Felix went to get away, but Mickey dragged him back by yanking hold on his elbow and pulling him backwards. The two toppled to the floor from the force that Mickey used. He was aging and old, and his hands were littered with liver spots – but he was strong. Surprisingly so. And despite Felix's familiarity with fist-fights and violence, he had not yet been to prison. Mickey had. And life in prison was quite different to the life led by criminals in the free world.

Mickey got Felix onto his back and, from behind, he planted his legs over the top of his shoulders to hold him down.

He then reached for the reel of rope that waited for him by the coffee table, amongst the stolen car parts.

He wrapped it around Felix's neck and each of his own hands...and pulled.

Felix tried to struggle free, his hands reaching up instinctively to pull at the coarse rope from around his neck. Mickey did not show any mercy, nor a single moment of weakness. He held the rope fast. He gripped his teeth and tensed his jaw. He watched with dark eyes as the writhing and squirming of his brother's body got more and more violent, more and more intense and desperate. And then slowly, steadily, delicately, relaxed into the sweet release of nothing.

Mickey held for another thirty seconds – just to be sure – and then allowed himself to relax. The whole kerfuffle had been relatively quiet, so nobody was listening through the walls, or going to come through the door. If anything, they had produced less noise than the other neighbours were currently doing. With their blaring TV sets and their petty little arguments – they were oblivious. The room they were in looked no messier than it did before.

Mickey did not act slowly. He grabbed the chair from the corner of the room and propped it up. He made a noose with the rope and tied it firmly around the light fixture. Then, mustering all of his strength, he slung the body over his shoulder and climbed onto the chair to attach everything into place. Felix hung there, swinging slightly. Mickey looked at him coldly, emotionless.

He grabbed a pen and paper from one of the messy drawers underneath the coffee table. And, carefully, calmly, delicately, and using his best handwriting – which looked very little like his own normal scrawl – wrote out a note. He signed it with a name that was not his own. He placed it in an envelope and left it on the coffee table, next to Felix's body.

"If you want something done, yer gotta do it yer fackin' self..." he muttered, irritated.

He went into Felix's bedroom and grabbed clothing that

he thought was naturally Felix's aesthetic, and changed into them – shoving his own clothing and belongings into a rucksack of his brothers, too. Before he left, he was sure to take the leather jacket from him too, right off his steadily chilling shoulders, as well as the sawn-off shot gun.

He then gave the flat one last once-over with his eyes. Happy with what he saw, he left.

With each step he took down the rickety metal staircase, Mickey felt himself calm. He was not anxious despite what he knew he was about to do. He was relaxed. He was calm knowing that the job he wanted to be done, *would* be done. He would ensure it.

The night was cool, but not frosty. Mickey walked the familiar route to the Brooker household. He decided to go through the back-alley entrance, that led to the back garden. As he walked, he internalised the things he had witnessed Felix do. The gait, the pace, the arrogant swagger. The slightly nervous nose-itch every now and again.

His legs took him there with no trouble. Before he knew it, the cobble stones were underneath his feet. The dark sky was above him; an inkwell of black. He could see his breath in the cold. It was calm, collected. The weight of the shot gun rested against his forearm. He had hidden it up the sleeve of the leather jacket. He was grateful he had skinny arms.

To his surprise, he noticed the gate to the house was already open. There was a noise coming from the garden, so Mickey was cautious when he approached. He was not here to disturb anybody else and did not wish to be seen. He was only here for one person, and that was Robert Brooker.

As luck would have it – that was exactly the person he was confronted with.

He gently pressed the gate, so it swung open without a sound. Robert was busying himself with his motorbike. He was checking various dials and mechanics of it. Mickey knew nothing about bikes. He was only interested in motors.

Brooker saw him approach.

"Ah, Felix, right?"

Mickey didn't open his mouth. Silently, he nodded.

"Perfect timing – I was just about to head out so you can do whatever you need to do. I'll just drive around for an hour or so, that give you plenty of time, right? The back door is open so you can just walk straight in."

"You're eager," Mickey said.

Brooker grinned a hideous, bright-white smile then popped on his motorcycle helmet, "I'm soon to be a single man again," he beamed, fastening the clip underneath his chin.

Mickey steadily filled the distance between the two of them.

"Any questions?" Brooker asked, a little unnerved by Mickey's stance.

"No," Mickey felt himself smirk, "I know everything I need to know."

He felt no need for a heroic speech, no need to explain why he was there or what he was doing. He let the shotgun slide out from his sleeve and he caught it in his ready, waiting palm.

Brooker remarked on the impressiveness of the choice of weapon. His chatty confidence then became fragile uncertainty as Mickey swung it and placed it underneath his chin. It fit snugly in the space between his helmet and the underside of his jaw.

"What are you d–?"

He didn't allow Robert to finish his last sentence. He did not gratify his question with an answer. Brooker did not deserve such things. He did not deserve to have last words. He did not deserve to have a movie-worthy ending to his life. Mickey felt good in the fact that the last moment of Brooker's life he as confused, he was weak, he was afraid, and he was not the fearless, macho scumbag that he portrayed himself to be.

It was seconds between placing the gun under his chin and taking away his life. He pulled the trigger and watched as, instantaneously, his head turned inside out, and the visor of his helmet was splattered with blood and gore and many other things. The body fell to the grass with a heavy *thud*. He was the slumped, empty shell of the man he had once been.

Mickey did not feel the need to hang about. He quickly grabbed the house keys from Brooker's limp hand, and locked the back door, before returning them to where he had found them.

Knowing Elaine would be safe, knowing she and her children could live their life free from fear, free from the monster that lived in the Master Bedroom, Mickey headed home.

He burned Felix's stolen clothes in the fireplace and hid the gun in a slit he made in the cushion of his sofa.

He was then arrested, interviewed, and released, once Felix's body and the note were found.

It was upon his release that Mickey took the gun out from the sofa and walked to the local park with it. There, on the bridge, he took it out of his sleeve, and dropped it into the rushing waters below him.

The bubbling foam of the rapids encapsulated it in an instant and carried it away.

CHAPTER 34

Some months later…

I t was summer. Mickey sat with Marcus on the park bench that Mickey frequented. The sun was glorious that morning. Warm like a fire in winter, but the space was filled with light and golden glows. The birds were ecstatic and were twittering loudly in the trees above, or foraging in the ground for bugs and grubs and worms.

The entire park was peaceful and filled with happy noises. Wildlife and happy chatting and the delighted laughs of children on the playpark.

The two sat for some time and spoke of the past. Marcus announced that he and Jane were engaged, and Mickey insisted on buying them the best wedding present he could – he just didn't know what it was quite yet.

They had had it out, back in February, when Mickey had been arrested. They had spoken of it, they had argued. Mickey had tried as hard as he could to not let Marcus know the truth, but his friend had successfully dragged it out of him in the end. He was grateful that, despite this knowledge, Marcus was not offended and did not change his thoughts of his friend.

"I knew you'd done it, all along," Marcus said, "I was upset that you didn't trust me enough to tell me the truth."

Mickey had understood his views. He hadn't told anyone,

or that was the plan. It was the best way to keep a secret tied down, and under control – if he was the only one who's lips it could pass through.

Old friends would always be old friends, though. And Marcus had sworn on his own grave that he would never cross Mickey – especially since he knew what Mickey was capable of, he joked.

"It's funny though really, isn't it?" Marcus said.

"How so? I don't remember laughing at the time."

"Well, the way it all panned out," Marcus's gaze wandered further afield, to the climbing frame with the children playing on it. Two dogs ran past where they were sitting, chasing one another and play-fighting over a stick. The joy that filled the place was amazing to witness, "What you did...it was wrong. It was unlawful, but...I don't know. I just don't feel like it was *as* bad as it could have been."

Mickey frowned as he thought and lit up a cigarette. He offered the packet to Marcus, who took one with a thankful nod.

"I mean," He went on, his lungs full of smoke. When he breathed out it came out in a wispy straight line, "What Felix wanted to do – that would have been undeniably bad, undeniably illegal, and undeniably wrong. And what Brooker did – he was genuinely just an awful being, in everything he did. He was hateful and wrong and committed so many crimes that he was never, and will never, be recognised for. But, you..." He took another drag, and his gaze was thoughtful and almost, somewhat, proud; "Even though I know what you did. Even though I know all the gory details. I wouldn't say you're a bad person. It's a tricky one, because you *did* break the law – twice – and I can't deny that – but...I'm hesitating to say that what you did was actually...*right*?"

Mickey was careful not to comment. He smirked at the kid and his kind words – despite the back-handed compliment that it felt like he was being given. It was not his place to say whether what he did was right or not – society and the outside world would, if they knew, make up their own opinion, and he presumed it would not be a positive one. He presumed he would be sent to prison again – probably for the rest of his days, if the truth were to come out – if the people were to know. But what allowed Mickey to sleep soundly at night was knowing that Elaine was safe, and that the world had two fewer evil people than it did before. That made him peaceful. Not happy – because he found no joy in doing what he did – but peaceful. The deed was done and would not need to be done again.

What it came down to, in his head, was grey areas. What he did was not entirely black, nor was it entirely white. He was somewhere in the middle.

He was not a hero, nor a villain. He was just a man, living his life. Making decisions that he was certain and sure of.

And right now, all Mickey was certain and sure of was this: he wanted to finish smoking his cigarette and then have a good cup of tea.

CLANDESTINE

Read on for a preview of V. J. Spencer's upcoming YA dystopian novel, 'Clandestine', coming soon.

CLANDESTINE (ADJ.)

Kept secret or done secretively, especially describing something which is unlawful or not officially allowed.

BEFORE

MANDATORY (ADJ.)

A compulsory action; required by law. Without dispute. I do not believe any of them wanted to go.

No one appeared excited here, from what my research has shown.

Any statements in the press from young cadets about the hopes they had for their shining futures were most likely propaganda. Yet this was what had to be done, regardless. This was the next step on their educational conveyor belt. Older siblings had done this before them, including Nia's older brother, and her parents, and theirs.

This was what was done, in those days. What made it scary for the new recruits, however, was how little they had been told about the experiences yet to come. Their own families, their own parents would go silent on the subject if ever they were asked.

The secrecy was unsettling.

CHAPTER ONE

128 DAYS BEFORE

They were ankle-deep in water by the time the bus arrived to pick them up. Despite wearing leather boots that covered her up to her knees, Nia was still soaked to the skin and shivering amongst the rest. The rain continued to beat down upon them ceaselessly. Their clothes, their conversations and their hearts had given up on the bus ever arriving. But they were too terrified of what would happen if they attempted to go back home.

The grey street was imprisoned by its grey buildings, which stretched upwards to the ever-grey sky. It filled Nia's heart with a sad, submissive ache. The water began to fill her boots. It made them squint as they looked at one another, oblivious; hopelessly searching for an answer to the questions they were all thinking: Why are we here? What is the point?

They knew only one thing for certain: they could not go home.

Not now, not as the same cowardly people who had left an hour before.

Their excuses would do no good. They were still only children. But still, it made no difference.

Despite their age, Nia noticed in the eyes around her that

the world had encouraged them to grow up too fast. This accelerated childhood had stretched the skin over their bones and drained the smiles from their faces. Replacing their youthful, joyful eyes with those of the common rush-hour folk – that look so often seen on the underground trains early in the morning, accompanied by a sturdy briefcase in one hand and a shimmering, commanding screen in the other.

The message was clear: the adults go to work and so they must also. There was always so much to do, and so everyone must always be working. There is a goal, you see. Nobody seems to know what it is, or where the finish line can be found. But there is a goal, and they knew they must work towards it.

The only flaw that Nia could see within this theory was that most people died before they got there. Perhaps they just didn't run fast enough. Perhaps they simply lost their way with all their speed, no longer able to find their way back to the path. No one really knew.

Those kids – there in the rain – they were nearing the final stage of education before they took their place in the grand, mechanical way of living. That is why they waited, with no complaint. That was the way they had been trained.

A great roar of a motor signalled the arrival of the bus. One of them held out their arm to signal it to stop. It was going to regardless, due to the amount of wet people stood huddled under the rusting sign:

CONSCRIPTION CADETS: PICK-UP POINT 6

Then, each in an orderly fashion, one by one, they stepped onto the vehicle and exchanged a single large copper coin for the privilege of getting out of the rain. Some of them were fortunate enough to get a seat. Others were not so lucky. They had to stand and shiver a while longer yet.

The doors slid closed with a mournful whine. It was the only sound on the bus. The driver looked blankly ahead as he followed his memorised routine. The air inside felt thick, and the windows turned cloudy from the warmth of the sardined bodies. Black puffs of dirtied air coughed and wheezed out of the back of the long vehicle and into the surrounding world. Nia watched it rise and disappear through the window. She wondered if it was really gone.

Surrounding her were bodies that were steadily regaining heat, their clothes drip-drying as they hung off their bones. If it weren't for the dampness, they would all have looked rather smart. This was, after all, an important journey they were embarking on today. So they were told, at least.

Beside Nia sat her cousin, Jay. He was a young man of a similar age to Nia. He had floppy caramel curls and a sly smile, on the few occasions that it ever appeared at the corners of his tightly shut mouth. Nia felt fortunate that she had someone beside her through all of this. They had been the best of friends since childhood. Whenever they could sneak away, they had frequently enjoyed playing in the woods together. It was a way to forget the seriousness that surrounded the rest of their lives.

As children, they had an escape. As eighteen-year-olds, they did not.

That morning, when they had closed their suitcases and their bedroom doors for what would be the final time, they had shared a very brief moment in the upstairs corridor of the house. All had been still. The clock ticked away quietly to itself on the landing and they had closed their respective doors almost in unison. Nia looked at Jay, and Jay looked at Nia, and each of them had shared the same expression. The unmistakable combination of fear, nerves, and nausea. It was common knowledge, back then. It happened for everyone. The two people who were leaving that house that day would not be the same two people who returned, three years from now – if they ever returned at all.

Without warning, Jay had pulled Nia into an embrace. He encased her. She was struck by how tall he now was. In her eyes, he was still the mischievous kid he had been when they grew up. To him, Nia was still the little blonde girl who had found joy in pointless trinkets like old pennies. That was what it felt like, for that brief moment, as they clung onto one another.

It was the childhood friends within them saying goodbye.

CHILDHOOD (N.)

The state or period of life in which a human is a child, often associated with memories of fun and happiness upon reflection in later life.

See also: NOSTALGIA and LABOUR.

In those days, life turned like a mechanical wheel: disciplined, rigid and monotonous. Children were raised strictly, under the same schooling, the same rules, and the same life plan as their peers, constructed before them from the moment they were born. This plan was not optional. Deviances were not tolerated. Questions were not asked, and – if they were – answers were not given. Everyone made the mistake of sticking with the same, stagnant excuse: this is the way we have always done it, for as long as we can remember.

This parasitic way of thinking resulted in an entire population who very rarely asked the question 'why?'. A passive, entirely authority-driven society. You or I might call it a dictatorship. Explanations were few and far between; and if it was a question that could be answered, it was done so with the assumption that further questioning would not be needed.

This matter was particularly true of anything to do with the Government. Nobody knew anything – not for a fact – about the way the country was run. The Government very rarely spoke to the people directly. The people were kept satisfactorily happy. According to the Authorities, and the Dictator, the people had no need to speak with them at all – nor the right to.

"Here is the Life Plan of every individual that exists, and ever will exist."

Education, work, housing, transportation, marital partners. All was mostly predetermined for them. And, believe it or not, for a fair bit of time, it worked.

The only choice they received in their life was their career. Once they chose, there was no turning back. Straying was punishable by death. Those who strayed or rebelled were outcasts, publicly shamed – never seen or spoken of again.

CHAPTER TWO

128 DAYS BEFORE

N ia looked left and right along the train station platform. Either side of her, in a perfect, orderly line, stood
the rest of the people her age who would soon be taking
the same journey she was. The line stretched for what seemed
like miles. She couldn't see the end of it. She wondered what
the others were thinking and wondered if it was all the same:
whether they were all as similar on the inside as they appeared
on the outside.

Each of the women wore dresses that covered their knees,
all in a similar style, and of various Governmental-approved
colours. Over that, a woollen coat, with circular buttons in the
same colour as the wool. They always wore dark shoes; brown
or black, and a beret cap to match. Some were not wearing
them today. Nia was too scared not to and preferred how it disguised the back of her head. Being slightly taller than the average female she was somewhat self-conscious today of how she
looked.

The clothes were comfortable, practical and fashionable for
the time. Truth be told, most of them did feel very smart as
they walked, and most certainly wanted to blend in with the
rest, terrified at the prospect of standing out. What did help,

of course, was that everyone around her had also been caught in the rain. Nia's coat, not being resistant to the water, felt uncomfortably sticky. It is the fine rain that soaks you through, as her grandfather would say - his response for every negative situation.

Shortly after an announcement over the speakers, the train steadily pulled in front of them all. It was as long and infinite as the platform itself, or so it seemed, and shone a glistening and gleaming crimson red. As a child, Nia had heard rumours about this train. On the schoolyard, people had whispered that it was painted by the blood of those cadets who did not make it home.

Still, no one appeared keen. Usual daily commutes to the offices or to school would consist of people bustling hurriedly, as politely as possible, all eager to be the first to step on board. Here, nobody moved for an awfully long time.

> And who can blame them? They did not wish to go. They did not wish to grow up.

Remarkably, as if they knew the crowd they would be faced with, the doors opened, all at once, all along the platform. Behind each sliding door stood a welcoming figure. A conductor, of sorts. Some men, some ladies, all smiling as if this was the day they had waited their entire lives for – and the expectation was that the children, too, should do the same.

"Welcome, welcome!" they said, as they ushered the passengers onto the train. In front of Nia stood a small but orderly line that had emerged from the crowd. She realised she was standing in line, and it had begun to form around her. Behind, she heard whispers and mutterings. She tried to believe they were not whispering about her or her family. She gulped. Part of her wondered why there was a universal aura of anxiety and resistance. They were scared, undoubtedly, but what was it they feared?

> What indeed... this is something I find so remarkable about humanity: if we decide to listen to our gut, and I mean really listen,

we can know such remarkable things while simultaneously not knowing anything at all. Nia felt scared but did not know why. It was her gut talking to her. It made her knees tremble and the tips of her fingers went numb and cold. Her gut knew. It was trying to tell her something. But Nia herself was tricked by the fact that the gentleman she was quickly approaching appeared nothing but polite and welcoming. She was trusting to her eyes, not her gut; and that, I tell you, is always a big mistake.

"And what is your name, ma'am?" he asked, when she was suddenly presented at the front of the line.

"Galloway, Ardenia."

"Ah, yes, here you are." He looked down at a tablet he held in his hand. Nia noticed he held her entire life history and personal information balanced on one palm. Her existence had been condensed down onto a single rectangle of artificial life. A rectangle so intelligent that it could recognise her from her voice, when the human man in front of her could not.

"When you step on board, turn left, and find the seat with your name on it. We've reserved it especially for you."

He gave her another winning smile. A smirk that you would expect to see from an amused gentleman at a dinner party. As Nia followed his instructions, she couldn't help but find his manner rather endearing. She began to relax. Lulled into a sudden sense of security.

The train carriage was not like those she had seen before. Nia had expected the conventional rows of paired seats, separated by an aisle, with windows to gaze out of when one's mind fancied a wander. This train gave no such things. Despite nearly twenty people boarding the carriage before her, she could not see a row of heads, as she had expected. Instead of seats, there were rows of singular black doors. They looked as if they were made of marble: polished and gleaming. The whole aisle was surrounded by the reflective black surfaces. She could not see in. She somehow doubted that the occupants could see out either. Upon each panel, which Nia presumed correctly to be the doors to the little pods, was another electronic screen. In white block capitals, were the names, birthdates, eye colours, hair colours, blood types and heritage of the travellers inside, with the same profiles and portraits as had been on the footman's tablet. As she walked and searched, Nia recognised some names. Friends from school, or children from the neighbourhood. She did not like how faceless they had all become, shut off from one another behind these doors. She later presumed that it was a way of keeping the new recruits separated to avoid any kind of negativity between them – be that negativity towards one another, or negativity towards the situation. Either way, it was deathly still.

Nevertheless, she found her name. She saw her own rounded face, long blonde hair, and grey eyes glowing on the black surface, and pressed her palm against the marble-like glass. The computer calculated and read the unique patterns on her hand.

"Welcome, Ardenia Galloway," said an automated voice. "Please take your seat."

The black glass slid to one side, allowing her to walk through into the darkness within.

There really was no turning back.

SCRUTINY (N.)

Deliberate examination or observation of the actions of an individual or group. Often associated with mistrust.

I would like to pause the story for a moment to talk briefly about Nia, as well as the others we are soon to hear about:

In my notes, you can see how every being in existence has an 'electric wall of information'. An electronic fingerprint, if you will. This is their public record. Their entire existence, personality, personal preferences, and history. It includes their likes, their dislikes, their physical features, their food allergies, school grades, achievements, medical history, their fears. It is linked to the records of all their family, as well as friends and work colleagues – anyone that they are affiliated with. Any photograph, video footage, newspaper article about them that ever existed is included on this page, in this electronic file.

Due to my work, I am fortunate enough to have been granted access to all these files. I have spent years of my life dedicated to reading through each of them, aiding me in finding links between the people we discuss.

However, I have searched and searched, yet one thing remains an obstacle. A glaring, black abyss amongst the facts, truths and testimonies that are the very foundations of my research.

According to public record, Ardenia Galloway has never existed.

CHAPTER THREE

128 DAYS BEFORE

T he pod was dark when she first stepped inside. It had a brilliantly clean, white leather chair, which Nia sat down in. She then watched the light from the outside corridor diminish as the door slid back into place.

It only took a few seconds before the lights turned on. It was a smooth action, which she found surprisingly calming. As was the voice which spoke to her next:

"Good morning, Nia Galloway. You prefer to be called Nia, don't you?" It was the same electronic voice that had asked her to take her seat. It was female, and very smooth. It felt as if she was speaking to Nia directly. "This is your conductor speaking. I am delighted to see you on board with us today. I know this may all seem very strange, but you have nothing to fear. We are all here to assist you today, and over the next coming years, in becoming the greatest version of yourself. If you require assistance in any way during our journey today, please press the red button on the wall to your right. This will signal a member of the crew to your aid. Please do not leave your cabin unattended under any circumstances."

The voice, which Nia correctly presumed was pre-recorded, signalled its farewell and left her in silence. She could hear nothing going on outside her little pod, nor did she know if any of the other passengers had taken their seats around her. For some reason, she felt like it had been designed in that way for a purpose.

Oh, how little she knew.

She wondered where Jay had gotten to and how he was feeling. Nia had felt lucky to know she had a familiar face beside her on the bus. Now, however, she was just as alone as everyone else. Confined in a cupboard of blackness, with a very comfortable chair...

When she really thought about it, it wasn't all that bad. Although her head had been filled with an inexplicable doubt, she now blamed it on nothing more than an over-active process of imagination. She believed she was not in danger, that she was going to discover the best version of herself, and that the people surrounding her would be the ones to teach her how to do it. They would help her find her purpose.

> She was wrong, of course. Nia did not know that this was all planned – that this procedure had been carried out so many times that those in authority were remarkably good at predicting the behaviours and movements of their young passengers, because they believed that young passengers were incredibly predictable beings. They were not entirely wrong, I suppose. Nia, after all, had gone through the designed stages of emotion that the Authorities had expected her to: anxiety, fear, loneliness, and finally, a false sense of security. So, at that moment, whilst on a mysteriously large train, hurtling at great speeds towards an unspecified location, Nia felt reasonably satisfied.

After all, she did have a comfy chair, which was supportive in all the right places. She had privacy and a quiet space where she would not be bothered. She had a handy storage space to place her one little suitcase beside her. The temperature was nice enough and comfortable. Later, she even discovered that at the push of a button her black box of a room could reveal a window to the outside world, or display a screen on the wall in front of her on which she could read the newspaper, or request a glass of water, or watch Government documentaries. It really wasn't that bad at all...

Then there was a knock at her door: a fast, sharp knock.

"Ardenia Galloway?"

Nia was drowsy by this point, and completely unaware of how long they had been travelling for.

"Yes?"

"It is time for your medical examination."

Nia was perplexed. There had been no mention of this previously. Nia was about to ask whether she had missed an announcement, when the door suddenly slid open and a smiling lady with afro hair stood outside it. She looked awfully smart: dressed impeccably, head to toe in white, and carried a clipboard.

"Bring your things," she said. "Hurry now."

Nia was flustered. Her movements were clumsy as she followed the instruction. She followed the white-coated woman down the aisle, clutching her bag to her chest. Not a single other door was open.

"I was unaware there would be a medical examination," Nia said. She felt a trembling in her fingertips. Nia kept her head bowed low and avoided any possible chance of eye contact, not that the white-coated woman looked at her. They quick-marched down the carriages. The reassurance and comfort, as to be expected, did not come.

"Oh? No matter. We are here now. You will have a full itinerary for your next week available at your seat when you return, so there should be no more unexpected surprises."

She pressed a few buttons on a keypad on the wall. The glass doors opened to reveal a very sanitary looking corridor, with entirely grey metal walls, floors and ceilings. Nia was marched to the next set of double doors – made of metal, not glass, this time – and again, more numbers were entered into the wall before they were granted access.

The room she stood in resembled the wards she had seen at the hospital where her mother worked. Only here everything looked insanely white and somehow even more sanitised. Nia noted white partition curtains surrounding and shrouding her view of the examination tables behind, then the other young people who lay upon them. Nia felt a flutter of nervousness in her stomach. Her throat tightened. She had to remind herself once again not to be nervous. This time, her reminder had less of an effect.

She was led to the furthest bed on the left, where another female figure sat waiting for her. She, too, had a clipboard in front of her where she sat on a white stool, as well as one of the electronic screens. Nia's face was yet again glowing miserably from behind the tablet's glass.

"Ardenia, this is Doctor Suzanne Schiffer. She will be carrying out the relevant medical procedures with you today. When you are finished, I will return to escort you back to your seat." And with that, she left the way she had come: a nameless woman, heels clicking on the hard floor as she walked away from them. Nia perched nervously on the cushioned table, facing Doctor Schiffer.

"Hello, Ardenia." She smiled, and her words were somewhat wooden. "My name is Doctor Schiffer and I will be carrying out your full medical examination today. We just want to make sure that everything is working correctly in your body, so that you have the physical capability to become your best self in name of this great country. Conducting these examinations whilst travelling will save us all time when we finally arrive at your new home."

There was a lengthy pause as Suzanne appeared to be waiting for confirmation that the woman had, indeed, vanished down the corridor. She fidgeted needlessly with the already-straight privacy curtain. Nia noticed her peeking over it discreetly until she heard the double doors sliding together once more.

Doctor Schiffer seemed to relax. Although there were other

practitioners and patients behind nothing but cloth, she was clearly more at ease and more comfortable beginning her work.

"Okay, let's get started." She smiled, looking at Nia directly. As she did so, for the first time that day Nia felt genuinely at ease in the presence of a stranger. Doctor Schiffer was not solely here to do her job. She was here to talk to her, to make sure she was okay. And Nia liked that.

"Now... Ardenia, have you had any abnormalities recently?"

"No," Nia replied.

"Any dizziness, headaches, or pain?"

"Not that I can remember, no."

"Well then, hopefully this will all just be routine."

She made innocent chit-chat to begin with. She asked Nia about her health, her life, her day. Nia watched her as she felt her stomach and tested her joints, then her reflexes and muscles. She took her heartbeat; her blood pressure; a sample of her blood. She looked in her ears, her eyes, her throat, and into her hair, at her scalp. Nia noticed as the Doctor did her work that the woman's hands were covered in very thin scars that mirrored the patterns of cracked glass: a spider's web of wounds sticking to her fingerprints and palms. When Schiffer noticed her looking at them, she rolled down her sleeves and attempted to hide the wounded skin from her.

It was when she was listening to Nia's lungs that she could not contain the question any longer. It blurted out before Nia had the chance to stop it.

"Why do you have those scars?"

It felt odd as it rolled off her tongue. It was not very often that anyone said the word 'why'. It reminded Nia of the first time she had ever called her father 'dad' instead of 'daddy'. When she first said it, it didn't feel quite right. It wasn't well practiced in her vocabulary, and she was scared it would possibly offend.

Suzanne's cold hands froze as she placed her stethoscope on Nia's back. When she spoke next, her voice was tense.

"Breathe in for me, please."

She most certainly had heard her. But there was still an exceedingly long silence before either of them said anything. Doctor Schiffer finished her examination. Then, with a tight mouth and anxious eyes, she peeked once more behind the curtain, before sitting back down opposite Nia. When she spoke, her voice was quiet, her face stern.

"It's just routine," she said quietly, "but you are not supposed to ask questions, if I'm not mistaken." Her smile had completely vanished. From her eyes, Nia could tell that her words were not borne out of anger, as she had feared they might be. More than anything else, she looked scared.

"I know," Nia said, unsure exactly what she was meant to say, "but no one has told me anything so far today. I don't know where we are going, or when I'll see the others again. This is all very confusing, and I... I just want to understand."

"That's how they rope you in," Schiffer whispered. It was barely a breath. So quiet that Nia scarcely heard the words. "They train you from the very beginning to be obedient, to blindly follow their every word... to be patient and loyal and submissive." She looked up, as if searching for some kind of help from the young girl sat in front of her, then looked down awkwardly and brushed back a single strand of hair that was out of place. She no longer looked happy and at ease, but instead appeared older than her thirty years. As if she'd seen too much of the world, as if her body and mind had been pushed to their very limits.

"I shouldn't be telling you this," she said, busying herself with papers that were already perfectly neat and filed. "You shouldn't be asking questions. Not about this."

Nia sat still, unsure of what to do. She felt like she had done something wrong, and yet Doctor Schiffer's fearful eyes were so compelling.

She shook her head, fretfully. She gripped her face in her hands and forcefully wiped a tear from her cheek with her trembling palm. "It's wrong, what they do, what they say. It's all lies. Remember that, okay? It's a trick. They don't care about you."

She stood up, her face firm again, as she finished her final medical checks on Nia. She scribbled a signature on her release form and ticked a great many boxes on the sheet of paper to confirm everything was working perfectly in the young woman's body.

"And promise me, Nia," Schiffer said, looking at Nia directly in the eyes again, "if you get even the smallest chance to run, to get out of the system, to hide from them before they start looking for you – please, *take it.*"

RELEASED OCTOBER 2020

Pre-order the eBook on Amazon, now!

ACKNOWLEDGEMENTS

There are several people whom, without their guidance and assistance, this book simply would not have been possible...

Mike, my incredible husband – never have I met someone as encouraging as you. Since you walked in, I've realised where my true passions lie. You give me a sense of direction, a bucket-load of motivation, and a heart full of self-belief. You're my soundboard when I have new ideas, and a wonderfully patient listener when I need to know how a sentence flows. I know you'd always be my number one fan, even if I hadn't written a book.

My family are also in need of a big hug and an equally big "thank you!". You guys have been my cheerleaders since day one, always told me I could be anything, and always supported me in whatever I chose to be. I know I didn't stick with the ballet and gymnastics and piano tutoring – but you gave me the world, and the courage to be whoever I wanted to be within it.

My oldest and noblest friend, Mel...who was so eager to be supportive she was the first person to EVER buy one of my books. You're an angel. Let's meet up soon for pizza and wine, yeah? Fleb. Wub you.

Mr Edmonds, Mr Stubbs, Mrs Critchley-Goodier, Miss Hough, and Mr Kerr: you guys were all brilliant teachers who all encouraged my writing (no matter how many short stories I shoved at you) and made me feel like my dreams were worth pursuing. Your roles in the world are so unbelievably important, like you cannot believe.

And last, but definitely not least – anyone and everyone who bought a copy of this book. Thank you for supporting my dream by purchasing and reading my work. I can't express in words how much it means to me.

<u>Thank you</u>.

ABOUT THE AUTHOR

V. J. Spencer

In the 20-odd years V.J. Spencer has been writing she has finished three novels and gained a Masters Degree in Publishing. Vic is an active member in the annual NaNoWriMo challenge, which takes place around the world each November. In 2019 she winged it without having prepped beforehand, and finished her first draft of 'Liberty' four days before the deadline.

Vic hopes to one day be published traditionally. In her spare time she enjoys vegetarian cooking and is currently failing to teach herself how to crochet. Liberty is her first self-published novel.

For updates on V.J. Spencer's upcoming novels, or to read her blog, check out her website, and follow her on Instagram:
www.vjspencer.co.uk
@vj_spencer

BOOKS BY THIS AUTHOR

Liberty

Clandestine (Coming October 2020)

Printed in Poland
by Amazon Fulfillment
Poland Sp. z o.o., Wrocław